Jeremy Cameron has worked in the field of crime for twenty years, the last ten of them as a probation officer in Walthamstow.

He also lives in Walthamstow, though he walks in Switzerland and plays cricket in Norfolk. He hopes no one in Walthamstow will steal his car, and to try to make sure of this he drives a Skoda.

There is, of course, absolutely no connection between anyone living or working in Walthamstow, or anywhere else, and any of the characters in this book, living or dead.

Vinnie Got Blown Away

Vinnie Got
Blown Away

JEREMY CAMERON

A Touchstone Book
LONDON . SYDNEY . NEW YORK . TOKYO
SINGAPORE . TORONTO

First published in Great Britain by Touchstone, 1995
An imprint of Simon & Schuster Ltd

Copyright © Jeremy Cameron, 1995

Simon & Schuster Ltd
West Garden Place
Kendal Street
London W2 2AQ

Simon & Schuster of Australia Pty Ltd
Sydney

A CIP catalogue record for this book is available from the
British Library

ISBN 0-671-71901-7

Typeset in Meridien 11/14pt by
Hewer Text Composition Services, Edinburgh
Printed in Great Britain by The Bath Press, Avon

Acknowledgements

With thanks to Nabila Khan for reading this through.

Thanks to Bill Clark for a vital piece of information.

Thanks to Caradoc King.

Thanks to Martin Fletcher and Jenny Olivier for all their trouble!

And finally thanks, of course, to my parents, Leslie and Peggy Cameron, who I hope won't understand a word of all this!

Chapter One

V innie was laying on the podium without his feet.
His feet were on the fourteenth.

'Vinnie my son,' I goes, 'you come off second best mate, you never ought to gone up there you fucker. Jesus Vinnie.'

He was dead. So would you be you fell off the fourteenth and no feet.

He was like a burst tomato.

Then I puked up all over him didn't help matters. 'Sorry geezer,' I muttered, 'sorry Vinnie mate only I aren't used to clocking geezers with no feet.' Then I had to kneel down I shook so much. He was my mate Vinnie.

Belled 999 on the mobile. Operator came on asking what service. 'Old Bill,' I goes. 'Quick.' Old Bill comes on. 'Been a murder,' I goes. 'Chingford Hall, St Francis, round the podium. Vinnie O'Rourke. Ain't got no feet on him they been sawed off. Jesus.'

Then I fucked off. No point sitting around waiting on

Old Bill. Be round mine soon enough. They knew Vinnie was my mate.

Vinnie was nineteen didn't know shit.

♦

Vinnie and me were mates since the time we found his stepdad shagging my mum. Brought us together like. There we were, let off school early some power failure, teacher brought us home. Vinnie said no one was in round his that time so teacher brought us both round mine, next block on Priory Court. I had a key let us in and there they were, on the carpet.

In front of teacher too.

'What you doin' 'ere Nicky?' goes my mum.

'What you doin' 'ere Vinnie?' his stepdad goes.

'What you doing on the floor Mum?' I goes, six years old, thought the floor was for wrestling.

'What you doin' shagging Nicky's mum?' five-year-old Vinnie goes, did know about some things.

'Excuse me Mrs Burkett,' teacher turns round and says, 'I brought Nicky home because there was a power failure. I didn't realise you were busy . . . measuring up for a new carpet.'

'Power failure!' screamed my mum. 'Bleeding power failure! And I'm not Mrs Burkett!' On account of she got married later on after having me and Sharon.

Vinnie and me we were always mates after that. Had something in common. Ask me I reckon teacher thought it was a laugh too.

Vinnie was dead.

No way he went there alone, heavy duty like that.

Or else he never reckoned. Went there do a small deal maybe handful of spliffs. Only he was out of his league, and me too.

I went off the estate puked up again. Then I went home for some grub.

♦

Over the footbridge on the North Circular, cross over Billet Road and down the Court. Mum was there and Shithead. Sharon was there with her kid.

'Well look who's here.'

'Where you been Nicky? Last three days your mum's been worried sick about you.'

''Ello Nicky,' Sharon goes.

Sat down and had a cup of tea.

'Vinnie was round for you,' Mum turns round and says.

Oh shit. I looked at the TV.

'What's up Nicky?' Sharon goes.

'Nothing.'

'Yeah, come round dinnertime said he wanted a hand. Maybe some sort of motor I dunno.'

'Anyone with him?'

'Black lad. Lives up Blackhorse somewhere.'

'Sherry?'

'That's him,' Sharon goes. Sherry was a mate of her Kevin, baby-father.

'They say anything? Where they were going?'

'No. Said to say they were here.'

I picked up the phone and belled Roy The Mouth was always my brief on the big stories. Nicked a pushbike you never belled Roy he couldn't be arsed, but you get in heavy bother Roy's your man, bit of wedge in it and he's there. Rang him at home.

'Sorry Roy mate,' I goes. 'Need your help mate.'

'All right Nicky,' he turns round and says. 'Got to be serious ringing me here, bit of time in it is there?'

'Could be big notes Roy.'

'Give it to me my son.'

'You reckon my mate Vinnie?'

'Vinnie O'Rourke, yes. Acted for him on a couple of burglaries, non-domestic.'

'He got blown away.'

'He never! Not Vinnie . . . Oh my Gawd.' Roy saw loads of future legal aid going up the canal.

'I found him. Called Old Bill. I better make a statement, need you there.'

'Sure Nicky, sure. We'll go up Chingford now. I'll meet you outside in half an hour, all right?'

But there was more and he knew it. So far there was no folding stuff but he could smell it out somewhere. 'What's the story Nicky?' he goes.

'Might be my brief on a capital,' I says.

'Ah. Now don't do anything foolish Nicky, you stay right there . . . but if you do anything foolish you know you can count on me of course.'

'See you Roy.'

Meanwhile Mum and Shithead and Sharon were gawking.

'Oh my God Nicky,' Mum says. 'Not Vinnie, little Vinnie.'

'Yeah.'

'Oh my God Nicky, now don't you get involved now.'

Rang a minicab take me Chingford nick. Then rang

George, my warrant officer. Got him at home.

'George,' I goes polite like, 'can you do me a favour? It's Nicky Burkett.'

'Jesus Nicky, how'd you get my home number you little bastard?' Then George remembers he's in front of his wife and kids. 'Nicky what the hell's up with you? You ain't got no fines the moment, you're all paid up. What the hell you ringing me here for?'

'George I need a favour. You being my warrant officer and all.' George summoned you to court you didn't pay your dues, fines and that. They made the good pigs warrant officers on account of it being a shitty job and how they weren't polite they might get sliced up. George had our patch, came on his pushbike about seven in the morning, had a cup of tea, sometimes stayed for a bit of breakfast then served the summons on you, court next week you didn't pay up.

'Nicky I ain't *your* warrant officer except it sometimes feels like it. I happen to be the officer covering your patch for my sins.'

'George I'm in a big one here.'

'Go on Nicky.'

'You know my mate Vinnie, lives Block F.'

'Vinnie O'Rourke.'

'He's been blown away on the estate. Thrown off the top. They sawed his plates off first.'

'Jesus.'

'I found him on the podium. Just going up Chingford make a statement. Can I like have you there as witness?'

'Witness to what? You need a lawyer Nicky.'

'I got a lawyer George. Roy Flowerdew.'

'No comment.'

'Want someone extra up Chingford.'

'What about your mum?'

'Leave it out George.'

'What about all them mates of yours Nicky?'

'They're all criminals. I got to have someone like straight, tell me where to go what happens next. This is big mischief George.'

'It's most irregular Nicky. I'm a police officer, I can't be your lawyer and I'm not the interviewing officer. What you want me to be?'

'You know them up Chingford George. Mess you around.' Couldn't like just say they straightened your teeth in the cells, he might not like it. 'And I ain't done nothing and I don't want no Chingford Filth saying I did.'

'Oi that's enough of that. All right Nicky, I dare say I'll wander down, say I know you both and might get information out of you, wipe your bum that sort of thing. See you there in fifteen minutes.'

'Appreciate it George. Do the same for you one day.'

'No you bleedin' won't.'

'Promise I'll pay all my fines straight up next time.'

'You could save us all a lot of trouble and not make it a next time. No chance of that though I suppose.'

Minicab was outside and I went up the nick. Insides shaking like, rattling. Sharon said she'd come, she was a good'un Sharon, but I said no like. Best get it sorted.

◆

In the minicab it was on the news so the copshop was buzzing. Papers, TV and the local *Guardian*, nice young bit. Met The Mouth outside and he was like a pig in shit, already put on extra lotion, smelled like a wine bar. 'Come on Nicky,' he went loudly for the TV 'let's get in there eh.'

First time I ever went in Chingford nick by the front door. There were stripes rolling up in all directions, Bill coming in from home on overtime, doors slamming, only at the desk it was like nothing was going down anywhere in the world. Shitty old walls, butts on the floor, one old geezer missing his dog, woman on a producer, Wayne Sapsford on daily reporting and some roller letting on the world was going to end at ten past eight. Duty sergeant drinking tea and taking details on the dog.

'Excuse me,' goes Roy being very important, 'my client here wishes to make a statement.'

'Be the first time,' says the sergeant. 'Thought all your clients got speech impediments Mr Flowerdew.'

'Now now sergeant, this is not the time for witticisms. Mr Burkett wishes to make a statement on the murder case.'

'What murder case is that then?' Mr Cool. But he went out the back and came back with DS Grant, fucking Mr Notorious down the whole borough. Two saving graces I had here, one I got a witness and two I wasn't black else I'd be head-butting DS Grant's toes then Assault On Police. Short, fat and liked freeman's.

'I ain't making no statement to him,' I goes.

'Let's see what we can sort out Nicky,' goes The Mouth. 'We'll go through and see who the officer in the case is.'

Went through and they found us a room. Then George the warrant turned up, not even his nick but he was talking to them. 'Thank you officer,' I went and got a sharp one, never called him officer before nor said thank you for that matter. Went out again and he did the business somehow and there was two came in, one young and thick, one older geezer I never saw before. Went to work.

Name and address and that. Been alone they'd have my bleeding prints. Got their pad out, one on notes the older geezer asking.

'Now tell us in your own words. Take your time. First, what was your purpose in visiting Chingford Hall tonight?'

'Visiting.'

'Who were you visiting?'

'Objection!' screams Roy, learned his style off American TV. 'My client has come here of his own free will to assist the police with a murder enquiry. His personal affairs are not relevant.'

'Went to see some tart,' I goes.

'I see. We'll come back to that if we need to. Take it from the start. Can you tell us which direction you were coming from and as near as possible the time?'

So it went off. Got to admit I shook a bit, needed a cup of tea. Told them all except about Vinnie going after Sherry, had to find Sherry first, see what they were after. Statement took up five pages then they read it back, didn't sound like anything I ever said but no objection. Signed it every page, they signed it and I was free to go.

'Please could you stay around the district,' goes the older geezer turned out to be DS O'Malley. 'You might be able to help us further. Oh and Mr Burkett, by the way, these look like heavy villains. You might want to keep a low profile, not try to solve the case yourself, you know?'

Otherwise I might want flying lessons too.

'Yeah,' I mumbled. 'Reckon.' Then we went out, thanked George and Roy lifted me back Mum's.

Wandsworth

What the fuck I'm doing back in Wandsworth God only knows. Down in Ford minding my own business and got a nice sideline in yeast, then suddenly ghosted out one day, pack your roll and you're back up the pigsty. No reason, don't need a reason. Discipline. The whole shit. Me a con near the end, hardly no nickings and back in Wandsworth treated like shit. Petition if you want, come about five years' time you get told to fuck off personally by the Minister of State.

Then they gave me mad Abdul straight off, aimed at telling me the score only for what I never reckoned. Called him Abdul, Turkish geezer, didn't speak English, spent all his time on the floor praying. Couldn't take too much of that praying.

Two days Brixton after court and then Abdul was here. Four years Importation some screw said, been on remand but reckoned he'd get not guilty. Had the trial, judge leaned over and gave him the sentence, Abdul smiled politely back at him and only found out when the interpreter gave him the news. Likely he never even knew he was guilty when he came in the airport, doing a favour some cousin, there you go a present for grandma and it's full of powder. Cousin bells the customs so they bust Abdul and the big one goes through somewhere else.

First night he got the trots, must have been nervous. Everyone got it some meals like semolina or curry only Abdul got it on special diet. You ever smelt special diet diarrhoea? Jesus. Probably not too bad back home only round here always reckon they put the yard sweepings in special diet, bit of dog end, bit of rat shit and chili it all up. Poor old Abdul, only it was me had to smell it all night out the slop bucket.

They put him on the workshop straight off occupy his mind. Sat there sewing and moaning, moaning and sewing. And praying. Only trouble was he lifted everything sharp he could lay his mitts on. God knows how he got them out the shop, they check all the gear and then they check the cons. Must have been a human magnet, got needles and nails and blades, the monte. And all the time moaning and praying so loud they had to turn the radio up.

So I grassed a whisper to the SO Saturday morning. 'Look Mr Andrews,' I goes polite like, 'you reckon Abdul's planning to have it away in a coffin, know what I mean?'

'Hah bloody hah,' he turns round and says.

'Straight up,' I goes. 'Only if he bleeds a lot do I get a single cell on account of emotional trauma because I just cleaned up that peter?'

They had to listen then what with the publicity, death's bad for the image in the modern nick. So they spun him, still never found anything, and put him on the topping list, meant they looked in once a night if you're lucky. Much good that did, next night he started sticking things in him.

Some of it went in his gob, swallowed a couple of screws (metal variety not uniformed) and a few nails and a plastic spoon. Then he took a needle stuck it right in his stomach so it disappeared.

Don't know what it did to his digestion but it turned mine.

Then he got a half-blade started cutting up his legs, thigh to ankle, cuts across cuts down everywhere.

I started yelling and screaming, got everyone on the wing going.

Times the screws can't be stuffed or won't unlock case you jump them although they already radioed the gate where they can't come out the glass and the other wings. This time the screw came up yawning, glanced casual through the door then couldn't get in quick enough. Artery job like a fountain all over the walls. Screw stuck a thumb on it, suddenly thought about Aids, took his thumb off, nearly got it in the eye, put his hankie on instead. Came in alone which they're not supposed to, other hand held down Abdul trying to slice his own throat so couldn't work the radio, yelled me to do it. Always wanted to work that gear so switched on and yelled, 'Hey this Big Daddy here, time to boogie. Come in Charlie come in Leroy come in Winston.' Started a full alert, panic buttons and got the Bill, even a chopper, then they couldn't touch me on account of I was being cooperative. Wouldn't help me get back to an open neither, though.

Carted Abdul off to outside hospital, the screw's hankie still on his leg. Tried to tell them about the foreigners in his belly but the MO didn't seem fussed so I reckoned either they'd find them or they wouldn't. Still couldn't credit that needle though, straight in never left a mark!

Next day chatted the SO about the single cell again but never got a result. Had to get me out of the blood but pissed off about the chopper so instead of the single they put me in with Wing Mirror Man.

Chapter Two

I was only on the estate for some puff and visit Kelly. Could easy buy the puff down the snooker hall but no harm killing two birds. Kelly lived on Sycamore with the kid, second floor, and first floor was good quality Moroccan. Only wanted a dozen spliffs for the weekend but it was quality blow, couldn't afford to pass it up. So I reckoned Friday night, put it up Kelly, buy some grass, game of pool and a few lagers up Hoe Street then maybe a Friday scrap. Bit of luck a few dickheads out of Loughton come up the dog track thought they'd bring the Sierra down town for a dustoff, then up Hoe Street for a lager. They were best of all for a rucking, dickheads out of Loughton honk up their rump steaks all over the gutter.

So I was heading up Sycamore Court when I clocked Vinnie without his feet. Never got the puff, never put it up Kelly, never needed to go looking for a straightener. Stand still it'd find me. Stand still too long and get no feet to stand on.

How the fuck you saw a geezer's plates off? For that matter, why the fuck? Only two reasons, either warn the rest or you just got a buzz off it. I could remember the days you just stabbed a geezer, now you had to saw his fucking legs off.

Vinnie wouldn't never want to go without his feet, I was sure of that. Poor fucking bastard. And only been shagging birds couple of years on account of they were Catholics. Poor fucking Vinnie.

First off I went round Sherry's that same night, see if I could find him, see what the game was. His mum came out the door, pleased to see Sherry's mates.

'Scuse me Mrs McAllister,' I went, 'I'm looking for Sherry.'

'Hey Nicky, where you been stranger? You all right?'

'All right Mrs McAllister, not bad. You seen Sherry? He was with . . .' Did she hear it on the news yet? 'He was with Vinnie O'Rourke earlier.'

'No Nicky, Sherry ain't been here since Tuesday. You tried his girlfriend on Boundary Road?'

'Who?'

'Tina Duffy. Little white girl lives up Walter Savill. I don't know the number but it's on the eighth I do believe. Might be up there if you try.'

'Thanks Mrs McAllister.'

'Don't you be such a stranger now. You still seeing that little Kelly?'

'When I can't get out the way, only she ain't so little now.'

'Now don't you be like that.' She laughed. 'See you Nicky.'

Knew that Tina, knew her well. Never realised Sherry was putting it up her now. Didn't want to make no

problems for him only I shagged her when I was fifteen.
That Tina. Maybe I wouldn't need to go round Kelly's
for a bit that night after all.

♦

I went down Boundary Road and up the flats. So
much wind in those flats you needed two lots under-
pants.

'Tina,' I goes through her door.

'Jesus Nicky, what you doin' here?' she goes, opening
it.

'Where's Sherry?'

'Sherry who?'

'Fuck off Tina this is important.'

'Don't know.'

'He's indoors innit?'

'Fucking take a butcher's Nicky you want, he ain't
here.'

'Where's he at?'

'Fuckin' don't know.'

'You know. And what about Vinnie?'

Her eyes flickered. She reckoned something, heard
about Vinnie, covering Sherry. 'Nicky he ain't here.'

'Tina you don't tell me where he is I grass on you
fuckin' me in the court that time.'

'See if I care.' So she already turned round and
told him.

'Grass on you and Elvis Littlejohn.'

'Fucked if I give a shit.'

'Riaz Mohammed.'

'Fucking bastard, fucking cunt, fucking . . .' So she

never let on about Riaz. 'Look Nicky I don't fucking know only he might be round Ronnie Good's.'

Now that was something else.

Ronnie Good was hard, Ronnie Good was the biz. You had a difference of opinion with Ronnie you kept it to yourself. Ronnie dealt for a living, but not big ones and he gave a fair deal, no shit, no aspirin and no OD. Ronnie Good was serious. Could have lived Southend on the seafront only he preferred his flat over the petshop on Wood Street. They left him alone he left them alone. Sherry maybe reckoned he was safe there. Only why did Ronnie take him in?

'Tina,' I goes, 'you got mates?'

'So?'

'Did Sherry tell you stay put or get out?'

'Fuckin' so what?'

'You got a kid then fuck off out. Sherry reckons he needs Ronnie Good then you need a holiday, like Ilford or Australia. Get a cab and fuck off out.' My good deed for the day.

In tower blocks I never ever got in the lift same floor I was visiting. No special reason except you could get a surprise in a lift. So I walked down one floor the seventh. Heard someone walking up quietly, two floors below.

I came in off the stairwell and went to the lifts. Pushed both quick. One came up no waiting and opened – empty. Got in there right quick and sent it down third floor, past the geezer walking up. Came out, no one around anywhere, like a grave sudden. I walked down the first floor quiet and went to the window, always open, reason it was so windy. Lifted myself up, spun round, took a look round and dropped out. Slipped round the corner and there out the front was a big shiny new BMW, dark windows. No one standing by it. No kids interfering with it neither. I moved off through the other motors and made the street, Beaconsfield Road.

Then sudden a mega crash came like a bomb. Up on the eighth out the window shot something big. Thought at first it was a body but was the TV – and video. Went through the glass like stars all over. Silence two seconds seemed like hours, then smash and thud on the concrete. Had something about windows these geezers.

Got Bill on the mobile again, second time tonight, nice to be in touch. Told them where it was. Not who I was. 'Better get here sharp,' I went, 'and bring shooters. It's them did Vinnie O'Rourke.' They'd know then it was me. 'Silver BMW reg K598 ARO. They aren't waiting.'

Loved a bit of bother the Filth, first there was thirty seconds, six more inside two minutes, stripes, trannies, meat-wagons, the lot. Only trouble the BMW did an exit in twenty-five seconds, they saw it go down Blackhorse screeching. No use trying to follow and it was ditched inside a mile. Expensive ditch, you could see it wasn't lifted that night. Probably a ring job though in the first place.

Found out later Tina was OK, only her video saw better days. These geezers, they seemed to bear a grudge. Not very sporting, not very sporting at all.

Now I had to reckon two things. Either they followed me, bad news for me and anyone I knew, or they went after Tina already, meant they'd likely be one step ahead of me all the time. Either way I was looking at a large case of bottle.

My game there were certain rules. Lean on someone smaller, don't get involved someone bigger and better. Someone bigger and better you gave them the floor.

Some kid outside the snooker hall you had odds. Three large geezers likely to hurt you, be very polite. Geezers threw people out of windows, used hacksaws on the punters, their business, always entitled to their opinions. No problem John.

Only this time things were different. Geezers had a serious attitude problem. First off they blew away Vinnie and I couldn't never let that go. Second it made no difference I went after them, fuckers were likely after me already or soon would be. I was involved in big wars.

The question was whether I moved up Glasgow or took them on. And put like that I better get some support.

Wandsworth

It was the chaplain suggested I wrote it all out. I was yakking on with him in confession about sin and that and he went how about writing it all out like, looking at it? Bit like the Bible he went, plenty sin in there, only trouble was I never read the Bible, preferred James Herbert.

Confession was a result, got you out of the cell. Not that the vicar's Catholic, nor me come to that, but we gave it a bit of chat Sundays. Cup of tea for that matter you play it heavy on the old wickedness.

Sundays church is the big hit. Nothing going down except maybe a video later so a load of cons take in a service. Best place for an escape too, you got a mind. Then again you can put in an app see the chaplain, only app you get Sundays takes you out the cell. So I reckoned on a bit of confession Sundays. Got to know a few spiritual problems mind, but chaplain's not a bad geezer, knows you never take it serious. Sometimes give you a phone call the bargain on account of the spiritual problems.

Matter of fact, best job the whole nick and that's chapel orderly. Better even than reception orderly or library redband, go where you want chapel orderly, no one touches you, just give out you're off on a service somewhere. Catch is you got to be religious. No problem going to church or a spot of confession but chapel orderly you got to be religious.

So there I was Sunday afternoon, giving it chat with the chaplain, let on a couple of burglaries, nothing too heavy, didn't want to put him off, moved on to football so he could show he was a man of the people. Came back on crime for a second cup of rosie and I thought we pop in the Catholic thing with the curtain, give us a bit of cred, when he goes how about writing it all down?

What, like for the news of the screws? I goes. Make plenty of folding then I could give up all this wickedness? Well, he goes, maybe he could beady it first, see if it was suitable, good for the soul of the general public. Ooh I don't know vicar I goes. Shit, if he clocked all that it was goodbye Sunday church, bit too wicked to be saved, banged up all morning. Ooh I don't know vicar I goes, might upset you, reckon I got to think about that. Fair enough, he goes.

So he lent me a Bible, reckoned it'd give me the general idea. Read the dirty bits, not bad. He had me down as a slice, next stop Open University.

Then just as I gets started they put fucking Wing Mirror Man in to distract me.

♦

Wing Mirror Man never looked a regular geezer.

Coming up thirty, thin like a Scotch wallet, hair longer one side than the other made him look always leaning over. They let him in the cell grinning like he knew something good the rest of us never. So I went what was he in for, like you do, make sure you never get banged up the nonces. So he grins again, chortles, shakes his hair and goes 'Wing mirrors again'.

'Wing mirrors?'

'I smashed five wirrors,' he went. 'Audi, two Escorts, one Nova and a BMW, yup! Then I found a policeman and showed him.'

'Right.'

'Yeah. Went to court this morning and got fourteen days.' Grinning.

'Fourteen days wing mirrors?'

'Yep.' Proud.

'You a persistent offender or what?'

'Thirty-one times in two years. Sometimes wipers too. Then I get twenty-eight days.'

Turned out he smashed wing mirrors every manor south of Brum. He was the Ronnie Kray of wing mirror smashing. Never got a gaff for the night or any wedge or just fucked off there he was away down the road smashing the old mirrors. Could start regular protection make a few nice ones, trouble was he only wanted get sent down.

He was due out good behaviour Saturday only no one gets out Saturdays so they reckoned Friday. Wing Mirror Man never wanted all weekend out there so he decided bad behaviour was better. Thursday breakfast he was out the line over the counter straight at the porridge. Tried to pick it up only it was massive so he knelt under it tipped it all over him. Might have been suicide if it was hot, only half fucking cold as usual and more likely he got set in cement. Rushed him off the showers up the hospital case they had to use a drill on him.

So he lost his time like he wanted and a couple days down the seg. What a road for the Big Sentence though. Drowned in prison porridge. Got to be unwell.

Chapter Three

R onnie Good was drinking Pernod down the Flower-pot on Wood Street. Well known he never drank only Pernod. Trained down Stratford with his boxing mates, drank mostly round the Green Man but had a nightie on Wood Street.

'Ronnie,' I goes sort of polite like. You didn't mess with Ronnie, only dealer never needed extra muscle.

'Nicky,' he goes. A bit like I was a packet of salt and vinegar, not sorry to see me not overjoyed neither.

'Pernod?' I goes.

'What you want Nicky, speed or Es?' Ronnie had no hair worth the mention and the lights round the bar shone off him.

'Bit of news Ronnie, you wouldn't mind.'

'Bit of news.'

'Sherry McAllister.'

Butchered me down his hooter. Ronnie didn't give you porkies, never needed to. Just wondering what the play was before he decided.

'I'm his mate Ronnie you know. I was Vinnie's mate.'

Ronnie got his Pernod. I doshed. He gave it consideration.

'Sherry McAllister,' he goes.

'Yeah.'

He wiped his mouth. 'You know I owes Sherry Nicky?'

'You owes Sherry Ronnie?' Maybe Madonna wanted my advice on her dance routines.

'Did me a favour lately. Hold still there a moment Nicky.' His eyes were past me suddenly, spotting someone came in the door. He put his glass down. Said 'stay there' sort of faint and he was away.

In the door was a man with a sawn-off.

Next him was another geezer, no sawn-off, had to be the speaker. Was about to make an announcement.

Both had tights on their heads.

Ronnie never waited for them to start.

It was moments. They were in the door about to shout, Ronnie was on his way over like he was just going home. Geezer with the voice lifted his head up, was half-way through a sound raising the whole boozer. A few people just beginning to register they were there and something was happening. Ronnie had the sawn-off, grabbed it hard, shoved it down, headed the geezer straight on the snout, cracked like they dropped a plate. Knee up the chin, had the shooter by the barrel, tore it out and swung the stock mad like a baseball bat straight up the speaker's eyes, too fast to see. Geezer screamed. Then brought it down hard behind the skull and he was cold. First one was no problem either.

'Mannie,' Ronnie goes to the guvnor, 'Old Bill quick.'

Mannie dials 999 and asks for shooters. Twenty–thirty people in the bar, blood spurting off the geezers, women started crying, first geezer was on the floor choking. I never decked anything like it, a few straighteners in my time only never anything like that. Ronnie was watching the door, sawn-off in his mitt.

'Shit and fuck,' I goes.

'Nicky lock this door, Mannie the back and side. Out of line the windows. Everyone else down.'

We moved. It was quiet, then more moaning and sobbing.

Then there was sirens and Old Bill was there. Counted forty by the end, eight of them shooters. Ambulances. Took the geezers away. First took the tights off. Faces were all messed, hard to recognise anyone but no one I knew. Both white geezers, probably Canning Town.

Old Bill was there two hours and so was everyone else. Women pigs, doctors for shock. Questioned Ronnie but thirty witnesses for him no problem, ask him down the station later. Fed them nothing, wouldn't feed them later. They recognised me as well and maybe half the punters there but had nothing on them. I could expect a search maybe tomorrow – a bit too much coincidence all in one day – but Ronnie had no connection and they never messed with him either.

They went and Ronnie finished his Pernod. Ice had melted by now.

'They after you Nicky?' he went, conversational. 'Them geezers?'

'Not so's I'd know.'

'Now they are.'

'How'd you mean Ronnie?'

'Someone in the bar before, got to be. Always have a watcher, see they do the business. Seed us chatting. Find out who you are, find out you knows Vinnie and

Sherry. See you leave. Come here after me found out I got Sherry. Now they fancy a chat with you.'

'Thanks Ronnie.'

'Mention it.'

We were thinking.

'What you do now Ronnie?'

Upped his glass, guvnor gave us both another.

'Fuck off out is what. Me I'm not after no war Nicky. Geezers are heavy. I don't use shooters, you know that.'

'Yeah.'

'Fuck off out till it settles.'

'Sherry?'

Gave me the stare. Then maybe reckoned well troubles couldn't get worse. 'Did me a favour Nicky. I got him.'

'Vinnie was my mate Ronnie. I want news on what was going down.'

He sipped his Pernod. 'Nicky you're as much use as a pair of goggles in a sea of shit. Fuck off out, go up Scotland or Wales or somewhere.'

'Vinnie was my mate. I need to chat with Sherry.'

'Nicky go home. No one chats with Sherry till this is over. We got something to say we'll get the word out. You got something to say you leave the word here. And watch your back out the door.'

He finished his Pernod and left.

Chingford Hall looked like it died.

I had to go back. It was raining and late and they were indoors watching videos and shooting up or making babies. It was dark and cold and Chingford Hall looked like hell. There was burning off some motor in the underground – you only put a motor there you wanted it lit up. Up against the clouds St Francis was moving. No lights looked like they were on. All the towers got their front doors locked with the intercom only you went down the car park and walked in.

I had to go back, couldn't keep off. Tonight was bound to be Old Bill up there and anyway the big men had to be gone. Every broadcast reckoned Vinnie did his flying out of the fourteenth, and Ricky Hurlock lived in 142, went to school together.

Went up the lift to the tenth, no one around as I walked up the rest. And guess what, there was two blue boys in 141, looked like they just did the class on how to look mean.

'Evening all' I goes.

'What you want scum?'

'Come to see my mate Ricky Hurlock in 142. Know him?'

'Who are you?'

'Nicky Corleone. Just call me boss.'

No one moved that floor or they wanted to know. One of them knocked on Ricky's door.

''Ello Ricky,' I goes, 'just came to purchase some drugs and a bit of stolen.'

'Oh that's all right then,' he goes, 'thought you was here to commit a murder Nicky. Come in.'

'Can I take a butcher's the other flat officer?' I goes to junior.

'No you can't. Fuck off.'

'Only asked. What were they up here for, you know?'

'Fucking gob off.'

'Yes officer.'

Went into Ricky's. Ricky was straight but he was a good geezer knew the score. Runway Ricky we called him on account of his sister Noreen.

Ricky lived there with his mum and dad and Noreen, never moved out, reckoned they liked the view. Ricky wasn't working nor his mum and dad, only Noreen. And that Noreen, not just the most beautiful bit of tit you ever saw, body like Whitney Houston, in the bargain she worked for British Airways, their West End office. Got exams at school, did computers then got her number at BA. Classy woman, cheap flights. I hoped she was in.

Ricky was always fucking off somewhere on freeman's on account of Noreen wasn't shacked up with anyone so family got them. Last minute job they never sold all the tickets and Ricky was off Frankfurt or Rome or somewhere. One weekend he went Antigua! Went Friday night missed a snooker match, never got the chance to bell us so we went one short, lost the match, beat his brains in after. Bastard reckoned he pulled his seventeen-year-old cousin out there as well. Wound me right up. Seventeen-year-old Antiguan bit on some palm beach, fucking roll on, brain damage.

Noreen was in and wearing a tight jumper. We went in Ricky's room and she brought tea and tequila.

'Noreen,' I went, 'like how I can get one of them divvies of yours for Antigua? Even settle for Marbella you like.'

'Got to change colour first off Nicky,' she goes, 'only family gets rates on tickets.'

'And what about if I like knock you off?' I suggested casual. 'You and me like, do I get a slice? Wouldn't turn you away you know Noreen.'

'Is that like a proposal Nicky?' she goes with her jam pies making my guts roll over. 'You like to get married to me?'

'Er well like yeah course Noreen. Well maybe not right off, you know how I respect you, maybe we ought to try it out first, you know maybe knock it off a bit see how it goes eh?'

'You're a real charmer Nicky, you know that?'

'No dissatisfied customers so far Noreen. What you reckon? Want to come down the club with me Sunday?'

'Ricky you're still getting into trouble aren't you?'

'Eh? What you mean trouble?'

'You know what I mean.'

'Mean sort of I go away now and then like?'

'And before that you steal things.'

'Well . . .' Not happy the way the conversation was going not romantic. 'Dunno's about steal's the right word Noreen, more like thieve occasionally.'

'Well you come back when you're finished thieving Nicky and we'll talk about that.' Smiled the big one. 'I don't knock off people keep going away or that matter keep thieving.' Gave it teeth again. Then sudden she put one hand right down my back inside the shirt, scratched me all the way up, nearly made me split my strides. 'Think what it's worth, you might even get free tickets you go straight Nicky eh?'

Ricky laughing near shit himself and Noreen went out. Tell you she had class that Noreen, I was in lust.

So Ricky hands me a tequila and lime. 'Well then Nicky,' he goes, 'what's the score? It about Vinnie?'

'Yeah. Reckoned you might know something Ricky, why they were here, what Vinnie was doing.'

'Know why they were here Nicky, everyone knew. Was a stash. Warehousing powder, bit of crack, bit of H. Lot of H.'

'Who's got the flat?'

'People sub-let, been gone a year. Pay the Council forty, sub-let a oner, you know.'

'Who they sub to?'

'They been gone too Nicky. Flat was empty three weeks. People heard it and came in. Needed a drop.'

'Good neighbours.'

'Frightened the fuck out of me man. Don't know who they were, you know I don't mix with that. One African, one Jamaican, one white that I saw. Meant business. Glad they're gone.'

We drank the tequila. It was after eleven now. 'Reckon I'll be gone,' I said. 'Come back if I need to ask anything Ricky.'

He looked doubtful. 'Yeah OK.' Then he goes 'Look Nicky that was fucking terrible happened to Vinnie, only them's mean geezers you know? My advice, don't go after them eh? End up dead.'

'I got to Ricky. Vinnie was my mate.'

'Sure. Only you get dead and that's just two dead Nicky, no future in it.'

'Thanks Ricky. Thanks for the tequila.' He let me out the door.

I went to walk down two floors like always, just a precaution, didn't want the light to show I came from the fourteenth. Wished the pigs a goodnight officers, got a fuck off back, then as I went in the stairwell someone came out the shadow and I nearly dumped one there and then.

'Nicky Burkett?' she went.

'Fucking roll on I near as shit meself. Who the fuck are you?'

'Remember me? I live downstairs, Chantel.'

'Oh right.' Chantel Livingstone, went to McEntee with her only she was two years younger, did athletics and sniffed glue. Dad was doing life. Mother was doing five.

'Nicky come in my place a minute, tell you something.'

'Yeah?' I looked for the exit. Heard she did scag now, no telling who was down her gaff.

'Got something you want to know.'

'Yeah.'

'Please Nicky, just a bit.'

'What you want Chantel?'

We were going down the stairs, went in the floor to her door.

'I got news Nicky, don't want to tell it out here.'

Made her go in her flat first and stand in the hall. Pulled a blade and waited a full minute then I went in. Slowly.

Nothing there. Stupid though, it was stupid and I went never do that again Nicky, never do that again.

'I heard you and that Old Bill. Hear everything down the pipes.'

'Yeah.'

'You were Vinnie's mate weren't you? Remember you at school.'

'Yeah.'

'Me and Vinnie we had a thing back then. Still did a bit now and again.'

So that was what he was doing up the tower. Fucking Chantel Livingstone. Only what was he doing with Sherry and looking for me?

'They had a big stash upstairs Nicky. They was business. They wasn't local.'

'Dealt you some?'

'Well . . . little.'

'For what?'

'Bit of this, bit of that.' She looked down. 'Did some lifting, you know.' Bit of shopping, bit of cunt, they were big business but did a bit off the back.

'And Vinnie got to know?'

'He was up here one day the African called. Went away again only Vinnie guessed, made me tell. Them was only here a week, heard it was empty. They made me a deal.'

'You went up and asked more like.'

Shrugged.

'So Vinnie found out, heard it was a big score and wanted some.'

'Yeah. But he wouldn't see it Nicky, I tried to tell him them was real mean geezers!'

'He found out.'

Vinnie didn't use, it was no good to him. Liked a bit of speed, even acid, but didn't use. Must have reckoned it looked easy dosh though. Take a couple of mates, even find the flat empty. Get the powder, sell it on. Maybe they already did and Sherry laid some off cheap on Ronnie Good? Maybe Vinnie went back for more?

Didn't matter. Now we knew the score. Vinnie was meddling and setting up competition the bargain. So he got dealt with. An example like, chuck him out only saw his plates off first. End of story.

Jesus. Vinnie didn't know shit, what the fuck was he doing?

Only I said all that before.

First I was knackered. Couldn't kip at Chantel's and never wanted to go home so reckoned I could go round Kelly's. Remembered anyway in all the excitement I never had the bit I set out for in the first place. Hoped Kelly was still up, anyway soon bang on her door.

Wandsworth

First time I ever got nicked was on account of that Tina was with Sherry now.

Till then couldn't call it crime really, and even you did I never got nicked. Started off ten years old, me and Vinnie and Wayne Sapsford broke into couple motors, few schools, like all kids. Most interested in sweet shops, weep now to think of it. There we were one time, did a sweet shop, took the glass, climbed in the window – could have bombed the safe, all we did was three hundred Mars Bars and a jar of green mints!

Made a few bob on the Mars though.

By the time Tina came along we'd built up a rep, fifteen years old, you got to make a living. Clothes shops and cassettes mostly, few wheels, few videos. Still never been nicked, though.

That Tina she was a right little cracker. Both of us reckoned we were the flashest round the estate and so I just had to have it. Got your reputation to think of. Well as that her mum had a house not a flat and it was rumoured (by wee Lennie, reckoned he was there at the time) Tina did it on the front porch. Up North Countess Road it was.

Definite step-up a porch. Very near indoors. Best I ever had then was a garden shed.

So Tina and me we'd been eyeballing each other round school and the club and the snooker, she flashed her knickers at me one time, all my mates were watching so I couldn't stand off much longer. Then one day I went in the Palmerston dinnertime and there she was with two geezers looked like they were out of Romford or the zoo. Never ought to be treading the streets of Walthamstow, blond hair and drove a Honda Prelude.

'Fancy a quick one Tina?' I went. 'And a drink first?'

'Who the fuck you think you are sonny boy?' went Romford.

Me and Tina ignored him. 'You got readies?' she asked.

'Near as.'

'Well listen Nicky, you get plenty I'll screw your little bollocks off, you hear?'

Seemed like a deal. Was a right little cracker that Tina, reminded me of the Grand Canyon. 'Be back later,' I went. 'Don't go away.'

First off I thought maybe lift the cassette out the Prelude and run it in the Palmerston, maybe back to the Romfords. Seemed a bit noisy though so I walked down Sainsbury's do some shopping.

Only one rule lifting from Sainsbury's. You got to run like fuck.

No problem nicking out the car park, cassettes and women's bags they don't give a shit, not their property only you really need a motor for that. In the shop though their dosh they're hot. Out the aisle two packets of biscuits in your coat and there's security, morning and please will you come this way up the manager's.

I got a bag first then two bottles of Scotch. Out the way I

came in, walked up the doors, security coming from both sides and I was out.

Ran like fuck.

Market day and they had no chance. I was up the High Street, in and out the stalls, half my mates were on the street (all supposed to be in geography) and weren't ready to let security past. By the time I turned off up Westbury Road they were well gone, history.

Sold the Scotch up the snooker hall on Hoe Street for ten, only small business but it was a start. Went home to get the speakers I lifted a couple of days earlier, fetched another score, enough for Tina now I reckoned. Then I went back up the Palmerston.

At this stage I still wasn't nicked, should have left it there only it turned out Tina was a very flash bird.

'Hey Tina!' I goes.

'All right Nicky? You got them readies?'

'Yeah I got them.'

'Who the fuck are you again?' goes Romford One. 'Out the way or I got to smack you.'

Not only yellow hair but he got a big hooter too. I got out the CS gas I carried those days, gave them both a quick whiff and they lay down having a bit of a cough. Tina and me we left.

Thought of nicking their motor only couldn't be seen in a Prelude. Walked up Forest Road to the cab office, went down Bakers Arms for a couple. Told her I'd screw her straight through that front porch and down the hall. She reckoned I'd need a banana give me an assist. Usual stuff, couple of drinks and she was panting for it.

Only it was still early and Tina goes how about a ride. Yeah good idea I went, back on your porch so she whacked me said not that sort of ride. Where you want to go? I says so she goes anywhere, maybe Southend maybe up the reservoirs. Yeah I thought, could shag her down in them marshes. So we got a kebab and she wanted some Babychams and we caught a bus on Lea Bridge Road up Whipps Cross, never liked buses. Walked up the hospital car park. Sometimes the Bill sat up there having a fag, more often no one around, better than the Central. Had a look round, all clear, lifted a Sierra.

In the Sierra no problem, through the boot on account of the later models they changed the locks on Fords, needed a hairpin now instead of your front door key. Sat inside there still no problem, Lord and Lady Muck. Only problem was I couldn't drive.

Been in plenty stolen motors only no one ever asked me to drive them away. Been up and down the Court one gear, been on banger tracks with Wayne Sapsford. The banger track though you were meant to hit things, Whipps Cross roundabout you were meant to keep out the way.

Tricky.

Made out to Tina I wasn't fussed about driving, just sit there a bit play some sounds. Only she went she wanted a ride at least home, show her mates. Couldn't back off then, anyway it started raining. So off we went. Put a tape on, ragga as it goes, revved the engine. What was the gear I went in last time?

Sierra was in the back row unfortunately, space behind but I never tried reverse. Got in second or third, banged the car in front out the way made space for us. Turned the wheel and we were travelling. Tina giggling like she had a tenner of blow.

Gear seemed all right, put the clutch down but still never got straightforward. Two miles home got there just over an hour, quicker by bus after all. And going by bus there'd never be Old Bill sitting there when I arrived. By chopper.

It was getting carried away did it. There I was in the Sierra, pleased as a fart and that Tina couldn't keep her mitts off me she was so happy, then instead of riding it straight home and leaving it with all the other stolens round the Court I had to try and show everyone, specially that Dean Longmore nicked a motor every day. Lived on the ground floor round Hillyfields so I reckoned it was cool leave it outside his back door.

Got there nice. Up Higham Hill Road like it was Brands Hatch, everyone very polite, got out the road quick. Turned up Hillyfields, straightened out clever only then the last minute I forgot which was brake and which was rev.

Still finished up six inches off his back door like I meant. Only it was six inches on the inside.

Little fucker Dean shit himself cackling when he found out. Meanwhile didn't seem sensible leaving a Sierra up their passage so me and Tina together found reverse, hoicked it out the way again. Did a bit of criminal damage on their decoration on account of they made the doorways so narrow those blocks, not big enough to get a Sierra through.

Then Tina got out the door, something about being sick. Me I never knew what to do now so circled out and went home, not far off. Thought if I went quietly no one'd notice, never reckoned on looking upstairs for the chopper. Always thought they were up there for the weather or something only this one was following me twenty minutes. Did me no harm in the district mind, it was like *Lethal Weapon*. Took the Sierra home, dumped it, tumbled out knackered and there was the Bill in six motors. Gave Mum a turn, kept expecting them to shoot her like they do on the news.

Never had shooters so they just had to give me a kicking down the nick. Got tired of that after a bit so they drew up nineteen charges. Did me no harm on the manor either, no one on the estate got more than ten before. Mum came down for the charges and the statement, couldn't make it earlier on account of she had the tea on.

There was Aggravated Vehicle and Criminal Damage and No Licence and Insurance and Unsupervised and Reckless and No 'L' Plates and a few others I never heard of. Then they stuck on Obstructing Police, knew I wouldn't go not guilty on one out of nineteen. Didn't give me a Producer, hardly worth it at fifteen. Nor tax evasion nor bullion robbery but enough to be going on with. Got my brief in, Mrs Mellow that time, and I made no reply when charged.

They reckoned I ought to get some driving lessons. Not many kids my age couldn't drive proper when they nicked a motor.

♦

Credit that Tina though, she came down the Youth Court and on account of we missed it before she gave me it in the ladies'. There we were right at it, her mate Karen standing guard, when the tannoy gave out 'NICHOLAS BURKETT TO COURT FOUR PLEASE!'

'Eek!' went Tina only not in ecstasy, squeezed me out there and then. 'Eek!' she went again. 'Fuckin' hell!' I went, 'bleedin' fuckin' hell!' and had to zip up and straight out the ladies' and down the hallway. Then Tina runs out after me, sudden cries out 'Nicky I'm leaking!' in front of all the briefs and social workers and runs back in again for a wipe round.

'Nicholas it is very disappointing to see you in this court,' goes the old biddy magistrate. Mum thought so too, sitting behind me going 'listen to her you bleedin' little prat'. 'Nicholas you are in very serious trouble here and we are going to ask for reports. It is our opinion that we may have to send you to custody. Do you have anything to say?'

Only I was shivering so much on account of nerves and getting out of Tina like that there was no telling what might happen inside my pants.

'Do you want to say anything Nicholas?'

'My name's Nicky,' I goes. Trust me say the wrong thing, then Mum whacked me for cheek, they should have done her ABH.

'We will see you again in four weeks when the reports are done young man,' they went.

And they did. Sent me away too, six weeks in the country getting beat up.

Never the same with Tina neither after that. We did it couple of times just because we were the flashest round the estate, only then there never seemed more point. Then she got a kid and got fat, by the time she was seventeen she was an old slag so I never bothered.

Chapter Four

I left Chantel's, walked across Sycamore Court, up past the piss in the lifts and dog shit on the stairs. Knew a man once got in the paper keeping foxes up his flat on Beaumont Road, tenth floor. Been on Chingford Hall no one'd ever know. Place was like a rabbit warren. Ought to make a rule all the Council got to live on the estate, soon get it cleaned up. You wanted to make a film life after the bomb just walk up Sycamore or Spruce Court one night in the dark. They reckoned one person in two got a record, one in twenty got a job, one in a hundred got a TV licence. Want a video? Step this way please. Want powder? Five minutes. Want a shooter? Back in half an hour.

I went upstairs, doors banging all night and smell the cooking through the pipes. Went and hammered on Kelly's door, only eleven thirty, might be expecting me.

'Who is it?'

'Me.'

'Nicky what you doing here? You can't come in now!'

'Why the fuck not? Who you got in there?'

'No one, see for yourself only it's late, you can't come in now.'

'I got to Kelly, get out the way. There's people looking for me.'

'Well they might look in here.' But she let me in, didn't seem keen though. That Kelly she'd been good to me, you had to say she stuck by me last time I was away. Nine months never slept with no one else or I'd smack her when I got out. Half the estate waiting to tell me. Then would you believe, soon as I got out, it wiggled she fucked it. Near as many as me I reckon. Fucking slag.

Went in the door and picked up Danny, two now knew his daddy. Grinned at me then slobbered all over. 'Hi Danny!' I went.

'Hi hi hi Daddy!'

Sat down and watched TV. Kelly had grub but I never fancied it. 'Saw the news,' she went, 'fucking terrible eh? Poor little Vinnie. There was coppers all over the estate Nicky.'

'Right.'

'Sealed it off two hours, went in every flat whole estate.'

'Say who they wanted?'

'No. Wasn't me and Danny no how. Never asked for you.' Pigs lifted me a couple of times there before, must have known I was down the nick this time.

'What you going to do Nicky?'

'Uh.'

'Them's mean geezers Nicky, you want to stay out the road.'

'Yeah.'

We watched a video. Did some puff. I said put Danny

to bed so she did. Then the video finished and she got on the settee lifted her skirt. I put it in her on the cushions. Felt a bit better after that. She gave me a cup of coffee and I went to bed.

It had been a fucking long day.

Been heading for the bunk-up with Kelly eight hours ago. Then first your best mate gets plated, second you're on TV, third some geezer with a sawn-off wants to put holes in the geezer you're having a Pernod with. Enough to make anyone tired.

I slept ten hours, got woken up by Danny climbing on the bed. Said hello to him, had another cup of coffee and pissed off out.

Went home, had a shower and some toast only never stopped long, preferred it Mum didn't get shot up. Called a cab as near the building as possible, got in and went down the Brewery Tap, corner of Markhouse Road. Reckoned I might find Jimmy Foley dealing crack. Me and Jimmy went way back, anyone give me information it was him.

Found him snout deep in a pint of Guinness, regular Saturday scene for Jimmy then down the bookie's.

'My man!' I goes.

'All right Nicky? Lager?'

'Don't mind. Need a verbal Jimmy.'

'Fair enough.'

We got the drinks and found a table, quiet. Landlord was having a crackdown on crack, you pardon the expression. Everything else in the world only no crack.

So Jimmy shifted some acid and a bit of speed earlier,
now he was on a pint of Guinness, relaxed.

'Where you get your crack Jimmy? Wholesale?'

'South London, you know?'

We drank a bit.

'Get anything off those merchants did Vinnie? Hear
they do crack as well as scag.'

'Them's scumbags Nicky.'

'Yeah but you did business with them?'

'Bit, you know, nothing special. They got an attitude.'

Say that again.

'Scag?'

'Never touch it Nicky, you know that.'

'True.'

We drank a bit.

'You hear anything on them?'

'Errol News, Micky Dressler?'

'Yeah and the other.'

'Andrew Okema.'

'Yeah.' One thing about Jimmy, he was never top
of the class. 'Yeah, you hear they stick around after
yesterday?'

'Yeah I guess. They got a big stash Nicky. You know
the game, come up south London, lay out a new estate,
make the contacts, get rid the gear and back. Not permanent, not their style. Could be dangerous only they got
muscle.'

'They got connections up Canning Town? You heard
about Wood Street last night?'

'Hired help. Could be Canning Town could be south
London.'

'Yeah I reckon. Thanks Jimmy. Owe you one.'

'Mention it Nicky. One thing though, them's big

geezers you know? Nasty fuckers. They still around, you don't want to argue.'

'Only Vinnie was my mate Jimmy. Yours too.'

'Yeah. Fucking world's coming to. Might have to go back stealing motors.' He laughed. 'You get one of them Re-start interviews lately? Reckoned me last week I got to show them proof I been looking for work. Reckoned I ought to said yeah, I looked an Astra up the Central and an Orion up Leo's and a nice new BMW back of the market.'

'They cut your dole?'

'Nah. Told them I was a brickie that was the end of it.'

'You a brickie?'

'Did one of them courses when we was in Feltham. Built a wall, fell down again and they gave me a certificate, so I'm a brickie.' He drank his Guinness. 'Only Vinnie's brown bread now so there's no future me getting involved. Got a nice little number. Gets difficult I go back to motors like I say.' Jimmy had a deal with a ringer, quality goods only.

'All right Jimmy.'

He finished his drink, went out the door and they shot him.

He came crashing back in the door, lay there in shock then ultimate pain. Landlord rang Old Bill, half the fucking street rang Old Bill, even punters coming out the bookie's, old dears coming off the market walking home for Saturday dinner. BMW went screeching off, Old Bill was there in two minutes pointing shooters. It was a long two minutes. Jimmy lay there screaming, I sat there shitting myself. Geezers had a serious attitude, a very serious attitude.

Learned afterwards it went straight through Jimmy, missed everything. Except he got shot he was lucky.

They reckoned you shouldn't ever drink Guinness before you got shot though.

And I sat there shitting myself. My number was next, not very far away next. Why they just didn't come in and shoot me? Never did understand. Waiting for me to come out like John Wayne maybe. Afraid of my muscle.

Ambulance took Jimmy off and Bill asked everyone the usual. Then on account of he was drinking with me and then there was Vinnie I finished up the fucking nick again. No fucking sympathy the Bill, all my mates getting hit but they spared me no distress.

Not a lot I was going to spill though. Give them the SP on the geezers and I was a dead man. Maybe I was a dead man anyway. It was time to take a rest.

♦

Had to nick an old Fiesta get over Stoke Newington. Other circumstances be ashamed lifting a Fiesta only now I had to be inconspicuous. Couldn't afford getting stopped, even checked the lights and exhaust. Nicked the Fiesta round Blackhorse Road tube, never ought to be parked there anyway, residents only.

Went up Stoke Newington to see Marigold. Marigold was brilliant.

Late Saturday afternoon never knew she'd be in, only I had to try out the borough and she was the only one I knew. Only one legal anyway, got no connections so no follow-ups. Marigold got a flat over some vegetarian place up Stoke Newington, got her own front door and smell of curry. I banged on the door, hoped for a long shot.

Feet came down the stairs and someone opened up. Stranger. Some bird nearly bald in some kind of diver's suit.

'Looking for Marigold,' I goes. 'This her gaff or she shifted?'

'This is her gaff,' the bird turns round and says.

'She indoors?'

'She might be. Who wants her?'

'Nicky.'

'Nicky?' Looks at me a bit closer like. 'Nicky Burkett?'

I was shocked. How she reckoned my name, was it on the news already about Jimmy?

'Nicky!' she went.

'Marigold?' I turns round and says.

'Nicky Burkett! What are you doing here? Come in!'

'Marigold this ain't you.'

She cackled. 'Just a slight adjustment to the hairstyle Nicky,' she goes leading up the stairs. 'It's still me.'

Four years since I saw her and she'd got bald.

'You mean it that way,' I goes, 'or you got a disease?'

'Yes of course I mean it that way Nicky, it's just a change of style.'

'Jesus. Where's your coat?'

'Well, it's in the wardrobe I expect, it gets a rest sometimes too, especially when I'm indoors.'

'You never took it off five years you were teaching us.'

'Well times change I suppose. Come in Nicky, how great to see you. I do see your name in the paper sometimes, I work in Stratford now but I still take the *Guardian* for old times' sake, just to see how my old pupils are doing.' She laughed, only that was a bit embarrassing really. They always put the court in the paper, shouldn't be allowed.

'I saw you in the *Newham Recorder* once as well, didn't I?'

'Oh er yeah maybe. Cavalier.'

'I don't remember the make of car, I just remember it was going at ninety and you went into custody at about the same speed. What would you like now Nicky, tea or coffee?'

'Coffee please Miss Marigold.' There it bleeding slipped out, talk of trouble and called her miss like it was detention. 'Er I mean Marigold.' She told us once her first name was Hyacinth only we never knew to believe her and no one ever called her that. Had to go for her coffee. Ask for tea and get all kinds of muck, big old leaves, probably better you smoked it. Coffee though was brilliant like Turkish.

Then we sat down and she asked what the game was. When I reckon we sat, I parked in a chair and she got on the floor. That diver's suit meant she probably just stopped aerobics or hallucinating or something.

Told her the whole story. Not why I was there yet.

Couple of minutes she never said a dickie. Then she looked up and went 'So you want somewhere to hide out a few days eh Nicky?'

'Don't know who else, honest Marigold. I got to get out the borough.'

'Nicky if you come back here you've got to be alone, right? No one behind you, no one at all. I don't want my place smashed up and I don't want to end up dead, I have a nice time in this life and I want a lot more of it yet, OK?'

She was brilliant that Marigold.

'No danger, honest. Sooner get nicked than bring anyone round here.'

'And you can't stay more than a few days Nicky, all right? I get a bit edgy if I have anyone around for a long time. You come and go as you want, but whatever happens a week's long enough, right?'

'Right.'

Then I reckoned something else. What about that Dirk? Bound to be aggravation he came back found a geezer there.

'What about that Dirk?' I goes.

'Oh, he's history,' she goes, smiling. 'He went back home, I still see him sometimes and I stay with him when I go to the south. I'm staying there this year on my way to Libya but he's not this way much these days.'

'He was one sharp geezer.'

'Yes, I know.' She grinned again. 'Right Nicky, do you want to eat something? I'll give you a towel and see if I can find a spare toothbrush, and there's a bed made up. Will you get some things tomorrow?'

'Yeah I reckon. You got any of them beans?'

She laughed. 'Oh, those beans. They won't do anything to your bowels these days, will they? I got in awful trouble with all your mums back then. Yes, I've got something in the pot Nicky, as a matter of fact, I'll put it on while you're in the shower.' Still telling me what to do.

'Serious.' Tried to think what else to say was good enough. 'Marigold, what you want for all this? Nick you a car, that sort of thing, jewellery, video?'

'Fuck off Nicky darling. I suppose you might try *not* nicking a car if you really want to thank me. I suppose that's too much to ask though.'

I thought about it. Yeah it was too much to ask.

Got a shower and a gallon of beans. Watched a video then slept eleven hours. Like she reckoned it was a bed only it never had legs, only mattresses round her place. Woke up and she was out running or down Camden Market like they do Sundays. Bread and honey and spare keys on the side.

Now I could start to plan for real, no looking over the shoulder all the time.

Never thought I'd be kipping in Marigold's gaff.

Wandsworth

We always went to school on Marigold's days.

She wore an old fur coat, never took it off, looked about a hundred at least, she reckoned it was artificial ratskin. Had blonde hair, almost white, stuck out all ways like she put her thumb up the electric kettle. Might be the style somewhere, maybe Finland, we'd ask she got her dinner hid in there, she'd stick her tongue out. Some days she never undid her coat we'd wonder she got anything on underneath, other days a flash of gold lurex. She got permanent aggravation off the head only he never could chop her on account of we all passed the exams.

She taught French.

We were only eleven. First time we saw her second day of term we never believed it. She was like off a *Mad Max* video. Mouth open job.

'I'm Miss Marigold,' she went. 'Geddout your text-books.'

Me I didn't get anything out. Gawped. Bright red spots on her face and biggest earrings I ever saw like blew about.

'I said geddout your book hairy.' She leaned down on me, jangling.

Shit. I got all the books I could get. Wasn't used to sarcasm off birds.

'Right?' she went.

'Right miss.' Quick.

She walked round growling. Couple started blubbing, Julie Seagrave wiped her snot on her hand only no one giggled or threw bits of wax out their ears like normal on a new teacher. She looked mean.

'Listen up bimbos,' she went. 'We're here to learn French, right?'

'Right.'

'And you all want a good time, right?'

Didn't know the answer on this one. Mumbled a bit mixed up yes and no like nes and yo, hoped we got it right.

'Correct.' She whirled round, coat flying, still growling. 'So we learn French or I'll have you by the short and curlies. And we learn French so we get a good time, right? And you want to go to France eh, you little bleeders?'

France. That was foreign.

'Only you little tossers have got to learn French or we don't get there. But if we do go you climb up the Eiffel Tower and ski down the mountains and see the biggest sand dune in Europe and meet all the sexy little French boys and girls eh?'

Shit.

'PAGE ONE!'

We were leery. Could mouth anything to Marigold long as you worked but you didn't you were history. One morning early she clocked Vinnie nodding off on account of he was out thieving all night. Picked him up one hand scruff of the neck, held him there almost arm's length till he woke up.

We worked.

Then a few weeks on she brought her geezer in to

yak to us. He was French. Reckoned his name was Dirk.

Not only he was French, he had a Harley. Skinny and dark like half-way Asian he had black shiny hair down his neck. Wore everything black head to foot, tight. Looked most evil geezer we ever met, reckoned he had to be carrying a blade. Came in right quiet, nearly made the caretaker swallow his fag then went to us about French poetry!

Made out he was in travel films although we made it drugs. Brought clips of French, showed us mountains and bars and topless sunbathers. And topless sunbathers. Turned round and said about organised crime in Marseilles and drugs from Africa and films and music. Far as we could make out France was total trouble. Marigold put up the school trip list, was the biggest party they ever took, people fighting put their names on.

Did more French two terms most kids learn five years. Got through first book in a month. Volunteering for detention so we got extra lessons. Weird. Head never cracked it, reckoned there was a conspiracy, kept bursting in detention find us scribbling away like headers trying to make out irregular verbs, thought we had a sentry.

Mondays we went to her flat. Lived up Coppermill Lane those days. Whole class there fighting for first, one night I gave Julie Seagrave a red nose trying to beat me, both eating our fish fingers from tea racing along Blackhorse. Flat was wicked – hippie carpets up the walls, incense on sticks and Indian music on the stack. Marigold made us meals out of beans, believe it, whole meals made out of beans. And chili. So hot we cried and one night little Wayne Sapsford shit all over her floor. Fortunate all the carpets were on the walls, floor was bare, soon got cleared up. Another time it was buckets of onion soup or baked bananas and cognac. Reckon now there was enough cognac get an ant pissed but we were cool. Then after the grub that Dirk showed videos or rabbited about the *maquis*. We were jealous of that bastard.

One other thing, that Dirk reckoned he held the world record for squatting, seemed he said all the French did it. Came in just squatted in the corner all night. One week we all went we'd beat him only we never got near. Fact Julie Seagrave broke her ankle trying.

Called it travel club, one night after it I did a runner, headed for Dover. Old Bill picked me up Elephant and Castle hitching a ride, one pound seven pence in my pocket and a jam sandwich. First time in a meat-wagon. Gave it out I was at risk. Only time I ever went in a meat-wagon on that, all the other times it was society was at risk. They reckoned.

◆

We went to France.

Marigold took us up the biggest sand dune in Europe. Fucking miles off, nearly Spain. Went in a transit, ten of us and her and some git teacher name of Moss on account they never let Marigold go on her tod. We went how if she got kidnapped we'd handle the van – Jimmy Foley TDA'd a Jag couple of months before. We got Moss. Wanker. We took no notice.

Rode Portsmouth took the ship. Nicked a bottle of Scotch and Wayne Sapsford nearly fell overboard only we let him back, last-minute decision. Then we rode hours and hours or weeks in the trannie down France. Rained. Ate baked beans out the tin. Then got out this sandhill made like Clacton and Southend piled on top each other endways.

It was wild. We piled out, ran up it like a hundred metres high. Well knackered. I got up second, would you believe first was a girl, black bird name of Paulette James. I got so riled I had to deck her, least I did when I caught up. Then we made down the other side and forgot all that on account of there were tits everywhere.

Me and that Paulette we just gawked. All that drive and knackered climbing that mountain we forgot all about topless birds being in Froggie. We just gawked. Poking out, swinging all over the shop.

They say you get used to it. We never.

Shelley Rosario topped on the beach, built better than Julie Seagrave or that Tina, made them right jealous. Got back home and she got to do it every Friday back of the prefab before PE, never let her forget. Gave her goosepimples in January.

Marigold never toplessed though and no one dared ask. We went like what did she reckon about it and she went fine only no one dare mention the next bit. Let Shelley do it and that Julie kept trying only nobody gave a shit, but Marigold never although Christ knows we cricked our heads trying a butcher's down her bikini. Was sure I'd get a wet dream thinking on it, not too sure what a wet dream was but sure I had it coming on.

Then four days we came home.

Slept outside the tents, got wet one night it pissed down. Played bowls the French kids, whacked them when they won, called them petits salauds, Marigold taught us. Went shopping, bought bread, cheese, peaches and wine. Never nicked anything. It was brilliant. Then we came home.

Got home van was a cesspit. Three days coming back no one washed, crisp packets, coke bottles, baked beans and old French bread everywhere. Someone puked and Julie Seagrave wet herself. It was rank. Kept the windows open and van rolling or it was oxygen masks.

Marigold said be at school next day clean it up or there'd be murders. All got there ten o'clock. Borrowed the hose off the caretaker got the tap turned on full. Put it in the front out the back, had the van clean five minutes, everything in a heap out the back. Then cleaned each other and Marigold and the caretaker and most the front the school. It was a burn. Never stopped laughing. Caretaker was all right only threatened to do his mad axe job, bury us under his beetroot.

Then we all went home got abused for being wet. Night before got abused being dirty, this time being clean.

That was French.

Chapter Five

Only I went in other classes besides French at school maybe I could make some fucking sense out all this.

Spent most of Sunday stuffing toast and honey and reading French books and thinking. Weird way spending Sunday, unless you were French that is.

So what was the play?

Vinnie got blown away. He got on someone's stash, tried a sideline. It was theirs, Vinnie wanted a little.

They got to make an example. That was Vinnie. Then again Sherry was around and he maybe had some away gave it Ronnie Good. So they made a few polite questions, pointed up that Tina. Made her a few polite questions, found out Ronnie Good drank up the Flowerpot. Went out making Ronnie Good a few polite questions – least they sent someone else out making them – only he was too quick.

Then they clocked me with Ronnie, asked around,

small town, traced me up Markhouse yakking Jimmy Foley. Put a hole in him. Next was me.

That much I made sense of. What I never made sense of was what the fuck I did next.

One way was sit in Marigold's a month then take an urgent holiday round China, maybe they finished their business when I got home. That was the good angle. Bad angle was they might come back again. Then again they blew Vinnie away, did I leave it? Jimmy, he wasn't that heavy on account of he was never my mate, only Vinnie though you never could let go. Got respect to think of. People got to hold you in respect or you were buried.

Then again I remembered Vinnie like that burst tomato.

Jimmy gave me names of the man. They rented muscle when they wanted only Jimmy gave me the man. Errol News I heard of. Never Canning Town wasn't Errol, wrong colour for a start, might be Stratford or south London. Micky Dressler I heard of, white gangster out of down south, came up here once in a while after some Securicor van. Andrew Okema I never reckoned. African. Not common have an African on scag, maybe he was the brains.

Biggest resident merchant on Chingford Hall was Brian Dear, retailed powder and shooters and wedding parties. Do you a package all three you wanted. Wasn't good manners someone selling on Brian's patch, he likely reckoned it not very funny. Other hand maybe Brian thought he'd fuck off a bit along Ronnie Good. Brian was mean only he wasn't stupid. They came in, found the pitch, scored, moved out again, Brian took back.

Maybe I could whisper Brian start a war. Then again maybe he wasn't interested. Only one way find out.

Belled him on his mobile. Unobtainable meant he took a vacation or he was humping some tart, otherwise business was being obtainable.

Got him.

'Brian, Nicky Burkett.'

'All right Nicky?'

'Brian, you reckon I was Vinnie O'Rourke's mate.'

'I reckon.'

'You know them geezers?'

'Yeah.'

'Wondered you were happy about it Brian.'

'Happy, not happy, for you to find out Nicky.'

'Just wondered Brian.'

We had a delay in the conversation.

'What's your fuckin' angle Nicky? You doing business or what?'

'Just wondered you were happy about them geezers Brian.'

'Nicky I'm a busy man, got an appointment with my lawyer then a massage, know what I mean? You want to do business, you know where to get me.' Then shut off.

Probably did have an appointment Sunday afternoon his lawyer, probably same time up the massage parlour slip him a few keep him sweet. Only one thing he wasn't interested was taking Micky Dressler. Never say only he reckoned Micky had a bigger weapon.

One place I couldn't go for an assist, or not unless the odds improved.

I thought on other powder merchants, never had any call for only clocked a few socially. Full-timers lived up Loughton got others bending arms for them, didn't often come up town. Part-timers more like errand boys, drove old Mercs, lived round the estates, like Jimmy Foley. I belled a few names up Loughton then a couple down Leyton Green. Always the same, you thought they all died or I got Aids and they never cared a shit about Micky Dressler.

Two things I wanted. One was spending so I could buy a bit of help. The other was the bit of help. I wanted some geezer totally out to breakfast and got a lot of friends. Some geezer slice you he never liked the colour of your shoes. Some geezer reckoned you insulted him or his family he remembered it ninety-five years and got God on his side in the bargain.

It had to be Rameez.

Sunday night Rameez went up Tottenham, up Joey's.

I went in Marigold's cupboards, see if there was anything besides bread and honey in the shop. Marigold still never showed and I never wanted to meet Rameez on an empty stomach. Found twenty-four tins of beans in there. Beans in jars, beans in packets, black beans, white beans, speckled beans, shit-coloured beans. Enough beans start a bike. Opened another cupboard – full of lentils, peas, barley, wheat, oats. It was a farmyard in there, middle of Stoke Newington.

Where were the kebabs? Where was the frozen pizza?

Not only Marigold never had a freezer, she never had a fridge. Soya milk sitting on the side. No margarine, no Tennants, no ice. Dry toast and honey and anything else you wanted you had to soak a week or two.

Only saving was the tins. I got a tin of houmous and a tin of callaloo and a tin of bean sprouts and a tin of bean curd and a tin of chestnut purée. Then a packet of fucking seaweed and some dry spaghetti and a tin of baked beans I found up the back and a few oats and some stuff looked like poppy seed. Tipped them all in a big pan like she used to make then set loose on the chili powder. Twenty minutes and it was something wicked. Enough for Marigold too when she got in, nice surprise I made her tea for her. Enough for six more as well, she brought them back.

I had two bowls down my throat, washed up and left a note for Marigold saying 'Marigold Your Tea Is In The Pan See You Later'. Then I went out for some wheels get up Tottenham.

Never liked lifting cars out the borough, never felt secure. Might be someone else's patch, get very unpopular. All the same was a couple of miles up Joey's so I needed wheels. I thought best get a granny car, being inconspicuous. No problem as it goes. Clocked a couple going in Spices, parked round the back, borrowed their Nova just when they were starting their kachoris.

Nine o'clock I got up Joey's and Rameez was due, regular hour Sundays. Saying I wasn't nervous was telling porkies. Rameez and me we still had a misunderstanding on account of I fucked up proper one time back, needed my brains examined.

Parked the motor, left it unlocked and did a deal with Joey's muscle, gave him the wheels for a free entry. Come closing time he'd retail it a few quid on someone wanting a ride home. Cops beadied it first was a chance he took, still never cost him. Needed a customer knew how to start a motor only most the customers at Joey's knew how to start a motor.

'Rameez in yet?' I went.

'Yet.'

'Tell him Nicky's here, like an appointment?'

'Appointment.'

He went and mumbled in his two-way and we stood there. Least he stood there and I shit myself.

Trouble was six months earlier I trod on Rameez's manor big-style. Got to be A1 mental to do that deliberate only I went and lifted his motor, believe it his personal motor, out of Leucha Road one lunchtime. Never knew it was his of course, only got it day before and never parked Coppermill Lane where he lived but put it round the corner. Should have fucking guessed though, K-reg Audi, stars and moons all down the wing, aerial twenty foot long and serious sounds inside, never fit the description the grannies on Leucha Road.

I was there and Wayne Sapsford got to be a loser and Vinnie. Just cruising. Audi was unlocked, started no trouble and we were drifting up the Forest when we found four shivs down the glove, reckoned then we made a fatal error. Went up High Beach showed it around then some kid Javed went it was Rameez's new motor. Could hear bricks of shit bouncing off the floor.

'Rameez?' I went to that Javed.

'Yeah.'

'Rameez?' went Wayne.

'Rameez?' went Vinnie.

It was very serious grief indeed.

Rameez lived his mum and dad and two sisters Coppermill Lane, went down the mosque every week, mother did a lunch club up the Asian Centre, dad drove the 97A, fuck knows where they got Rameez. Sisters fucking beautiful, give either a quick one only they went home seven o'clock, give you the eye and that was it. Anyway touch one and Rameez likely slice your ear off. Fact you do anything else irritated him he sliced your ear off. Three in the borough already the last count. Better you were on the right side of him. Better you never lifted his day-old Audi.

Six months now I was staying out all dark corners. Rushed his motor back, left a note under the wipers 'sorry Rameez didn't reckon it yours honest mate, honest' then fucked off quick. Seen him once in the distance, made off direction Glasgow. Heard he was on my case.

Now he came out the foyer with his buddies.

'Nicky Burkett,' he goes.

'Rameez, good to clock you mate.'

'Nicky Burkett you owes me three-quarters of a gallon of unleaded fuel.'

'Any time Rameez, I pays my debts. Reckon an apology too.'

'That why you here?'

'Yeah. Well, that and a bit.'

'What the bit Nicky Burkett?' His buddies were looking restive like they were hungry or they never drew blood that evening.

'Rameez, I got a business proposal I think you might be interested. Fact is needs a geezer bigger than me. Personal matter only could be big readies in it. I need your assist.'

He gave me the gaze like I was a Scouser or carried a dangerous disease. Slow and nasty.

'You need my assist? You fuckin' want my assist?'

'Fact is Rameez, you're the only feller big enough for this game. No one else the borough, I never offered it no one.'

Gave me the slow and nasty again. Still not made up about his Audi.

Then sudden he cleared his mind. Gave it teeth. Went, 'Right Nicky Burkett, you tell me the score man and I think about it. Come through the bar, sit down, tell me the score.'

We went through the bar, me and Rameez and all his buddies. Me and Rameez sat by the bar, buddies stood around looking important. Three hundred people in there, din like the business, deals all over. Was where Rameez went Sundays get his stock for the week. Got it dead cheap not very surprising. Did his work off ringers and a bit of protection, minicabs and take-aways round Blackhorse and Markhouse. Never dealt gear, bought it regulation except half regulation price. Now he let me buy him a Bacardi.

'Give it me Nicky Burkett,' he shouted over the din. 'Sell it to me man.'

'Tell you the whole score Rameez,' I shouted.

'Tell me the whole score Nicky Burkett.'

We paused, give the meeting the seriousness it deserved. Then I started. Sat up straight, cleared the throat and yelled serious.

'You reckon my mate Vinnie got sawed?'

'Yeah I heard. I'm sorry. We're all sorry.'

'All sorry,' went his buddies, five yards away heard everything on account we were shouting.

'You heard who done it?'

'Nah.'

Seemed a bit unlikely he heard nothing. Then again maybe he could get peeved it never reached him. 'What it never reached you Rameez?' I goes.

'Never reached me Nicky Burkett. I stay out the way I'm not involved.'

'They're big people Rameez.'

'Like who?'

'Like Errol News.'

'Quite big Errol News.'

'Like Micky Dressler.'

'Quite very big Micky Dressler.'

'Like Andrew Okema.'

'Quite like I never heard of him.'

'Me neither.'

'And they got muscle too?'

'Plenty. Two shootings you heard of, Flowerpot and Brewery Tap. Flat up Walter Savill they smashed up.'

'So that's two quite big geezers Nicky Burkett and one we never made, and they got plenty muscle and they disturbing the peace of our neighbourhood. What their game or do I guess?'

'Large gear dump. Move in, clear out on Class A, move out. No interference off the locals. Brian Dear, on his patch but he don't want to know. Ronnie Good, not interested, take a holiday. They move in our manor, disturb the peace of our neighbourhood like you say, make our kids into junkies, move out again and ain't no one there to protect the kids and hold up our honour.' Rameez was big on honour, I reckoned that, and peace round the neighbourhood according to him.

''Cept your mate Vinnie?'

'Like to say that Rameez, like to say that. Be straight with you though he was up after a freeman's fuckin' soft idiot. They made an example.'

Rameez whistled. Least it looked like he did, we shouted everything else only I never heard the whistle over the din. He whistled quiet. Maybe they put a few ideas in his bonce how to make examples. He sipped his

Bacardi. His buddies sipped their Bacardis, looked like they were thinking.

'Nicky Burkett, what you got in it for me?'

'Two deals Rameez. One I give you the way on a bit of work, good payment. Very good payment.'

He looked quiet.

'Two you got your honour. Clean up the borough makes you the lord, no one in your league. And you keep the streets clean for our kids and your family.'

Still looked quiet. Knew I couldn't give him details on the first or he'd have it away. Needed a commitment off him. The second was the taster, still wouldn't go without payment but the honour was it.

He finished his Bacardi, got off his stool. Some blonde bit was walking his way flashing her tits at him. His time for a feel.

'Nicky Burkett,' he shouts, 'we have a meeting Tuesday down the Standard, nine o'clock and I give you my opinion. Right?'

'Right.' I looked honourable. 'And I owe you Rameez.'

'You don't owe me fuckin' nothing Nicky Burkett, except three quarters of a gallon unleaded fuel. I ain't agreed nothing yet and I do you still don't owe me. Do it if I want. You have the deal ready though eh?'

'Have the deal.' He was gone after the blonde bit.

Now I had to dream up some fucking deal on the first part the bargain.

Wandsworth

There's worse than this nick. Go up north you reckon London nicks are fucking massage parlours. But still you can get the fever just staring at the walls. You got to find ways to manage.

Remand's the worst, some nicks got twenty-three-hour bang-up. Make it even worse you don't even know you get a guilty, let alone you get a squeeze or a long one. Best on remand's strike time, screws won't accept any more in the nick so you go off the police cells, give you TV all night and take-away pizza. Only trouble is you finish up some place like Grimsby they never even heard of pizza.

Then after court you get Wandsworth or Pentonville and more bang-up. Pentonville they treat you all right, Wandsworth like shit. Even visitors they treat like shit up Wandsworth. No work except a few lickers or maybe you're a master chef or something so stare at the walls again. Good job they got the drugs. Brixton used to be best on account of it was all remands and daily visits, hardly get down the corridors for smoke. Now Wandsworth and Pentonville both got remands and long sentences everyone's happy. More crack than on the street. Me, I don't use it, anyway so stoned most the time I couldn't hold my hooter straight. Fair quality spliff in here right now you got to say.

Then again we get a little drink-up weekends. Not like the long-terms, Lartin or Parkhurst you get a real party, but could be worse. Got to have a bit of care, some of the liquor make you go blind but I had worse out the offie. Old cons reckon the old days they made the liquor in slop buckets and cisterns. Fuck that. Nowadays you can always get the draw so you only use liquor if conditions are fair. You got the yeast out the kitchens, you got anything else you need only no hops. Shame about no hops, drive a man on the hard liquor only some reason you never can get hops in nick.

Got to manage whatever.

Too much time thinking and you're out of it. Jacket job. Reckon you got the master plan never get nicked again or beat your woman, go self-employed painting and decorating or rob a bullion. All night every night thinking on the master plan, never get sleep, lose three stone, then it's down F wing Brixton, in with the schizos. Then you get out and it's the same as before, no work decorating or anything else that matter, beat your woman first time she steps out of line or maybe second, look out an earner and get nicked legging it out the chemist's. Better off not doing all that thinking. Don't make any fucking difference.

So there's books in here, there's work if you're lucky, there's radios and personals and fucking scrabble and gym twice a week means extra showers. You got private spends there's papers. You buy your toiletries and batteries, only you wire up on the light bulb you don't get nicked. Association twice a week gets you TV up till bang-up eight o'clock. Could be worse only I never want to throw a wobbler so I do classes, keep occupied. French and guitar. Some nicks spend millions on workshops and classrooms then there's no machinery or teachers.

This nick there's teachers, go in education spend forty minutes looking up their legs. Guitar teacher's a rasta though, all the black geezers want the weed off him only he goes artificial stimulation that's bad for the brain so there's a lot of geezers only take guitar one lesson.

Then there's the chat.

All of them millionaires in here. Every John got a stash outside, few Ks, Roller, some piece sequins up her fanny, jobs lined up and likely a penthouse in the bargain. None of them on the doss and all of them only inside on account of they got grassed up one job.

Take no notice me. Sometimes it's a cream, sometimes it's a fuck-up. Knew a geezer Jason Debrett, broke in a builder's merchant down Leyton, have a sniff around nothing special, found the safe open and ten thou lying there new notes. Never worried where it came from or why the safe was open, lifted it, spent it in a week. Never heard a dicky. Most likely there was big geezers going round shafting each other on account of it was part some arrangement. No one thought ask a few little ones round Jason Debrett. Was a wanker that Jase, let on everyone he ever met, lucky he never got plunged even for what was up his back pocket never mind the big geezers felt aggravated. Only he got fortunate.

Other times step out home going down the snooker club you get lifted going equipped. Just on account of you got a screwdriver in your jacket and glancing the motors on Hoe Street. Never a geezer in Walthamstow hasn't got a screwdriver down his jacket and looking up some Audi he sees one, hardly go interfering on Hoe Street only being it's me the Bill reckon they like to show me the inside of a cell case I forgot what it looks like.

You take it you leave it. Sometimes it goes, sometimes it's a fuck-up. Mind you I still got grassed up plenty otherwise I never saw all these gaffs. Only at the end of it I never reckon it wasn't for getting grassed up I'd be cruising down California shagging Madonna.

They reckon successful cons are all on the Costa del Job only I wouldn't know. Round here there's plenty reckon they're successful cons or least they're working on it, nineteen-year-olds reckon they're Yardies, can't understand why they're only here temporarily on their way some youth prison. Listen up on the bits of work done by cons in here you never thought there was a Sierra left on the streets or a Securicor van still running. Then when they get out that Bank of England's got a hard time coming and all those krugerrands up Thiefrow. So much blah, nobody favours getting nicked so there's mouth like there's no tomorrow.

Course there's some barons in here only not what you'd call real barons. Real barons get banged up in real barons' gaffs. Round here you get some passing through and you leave them alone, only our part-time barons are mostly who's got the best connections on the draw. Good supply makes all kinds into barons, regular visits or maybe backhand a screw bring some in. There's some screw give you the brief on a spin coming up, maybe even hold the gear for you till it's gone. Whatever, it's the supply and the stash makes barons.

Leave aside the Class A, means serious warfare, leave that right out. Most cons only need the draw get through their sentence, we all want to stay loose so we pay the dues, cigs and toiletries and cash, and get the gear. No cash in prison, that's official. Last Sunday visit I clocked a fortnight's weed come in and £750 go out. Sunday's best on visits, more people around. Screws know what goes down anyway so now and again you get a strip but mostly they want a quiet nick so you get the gear. Get done and maybe lose twenty-eight days, worth it for the cash and some smoke.

Me I stay cool. Don't come on strong don't cry about it. Can't do the time, don't do the crime. Cracks you up, might as well admit it, but got to manage. Come twenty-five or thirty you never want to be in nick much more, unless you land a big one then it might be worth it. Best is land a big one and never get nicked, then you can afford to go straight even.

Meanwhile you got to manage. There are geezers learn to do two thousand press-ups on one finger and geezers on Open University Criminology reckon that's a doss. Me though like most cons I get by on a bit of gym and classes and whacking the nonces and best of all like I said is chapel orderly you can get it. You want to get outside the nick though, pass a bit of time, you either get on the works or some nicks you get local college is a main result. Failing that go for the football team.

Generally they play against teams in outside leagues. Special arrangements all matches are at home, shame that, only you get oranges half time, showers, even extra grub build you up. Depends on the screw in charge. Then again sometimes there's someone's mate on the visitors slips you a bit of snout, even weed. Have to take a plastic bag mind, swallow it on the pitch on account of they search regular before you get back on the wing. Best of all though you get off workshops training and no loss of earnings, and weekends you get off the wing all afternoon. You just got to be a footballer.

Me I'm no footballer. No skill. Never mind a game only

there's good players I can go home. Early on though I knew I had to get in the squad any nick I was in so there had to be other ways. Decided it had to be the axeman.

I was the chopper. Maniac. Ripper.

Most cons are shit soft. There's exceptions, like I say, and you got to know them. Hard men you don't aggravate in the recess, fact you don't go anywhere near the recess they're there case they don't like the shape of your ears, want to change them. Then there's scrappers – loads of them just enjoy a scrap, doesn't mean they're hard. Most cons are shit soft and most footballers are shit soft. Real footballers are hard, never mind what it looks like on TV, only real footballers only come in nick like once in a while – Tony Adams or that Peter Storey. And even scrappers generally get leery on a pitch when they reckon there's a maniac around. So I was the maniac.

Didn't really suit all that running about being hard. Worth it though get out of the cell. Even the oranges.

First you got to impress.

Bounce out the cell on unlock, breezy and sharp and that, rub the chest you want. 'Morning officer,' you go, whatever shithead unlocks you. 'Nice day good game of football eh?' Never reckoned screws being all that sharp, liked getting their arses licked whatever.

Then you never got to give grief, that is unless you played Tottenham then you do what the fuck you feel like. Me I never did give grief, get the time done. 'Morning officer,' I go when there's football poncing down the wing see the PO or SO on the centre, 'any good jobs coming up? Cleaner, laundry, toilet operative?'

Then there's the gym get noticed. All regular sessions and any extras there's me pumping iron. Strictly for men and magazines that pumping game only you got to do a bit. Need supplements do that properly on account of the food in nick's got no nutrition so you get an excuse give up after a bit. Got to do circuits though, you never do circuits they reckon you're not serious. Last of all there's the ball skills. Ball skills is where you establish your rep.

Best you never look at the ball. Practise ball skills in sixes you make your mark on all six of them. Between the knee and the shoulder same as real life so there's nothing shows and you never get charged assault. They reckon it never hurts you get it in first. Bollocks. Depends how much you want to get out the cell. First time I was the chopper on sixes I got back lay down, had bruises all over like a junkie. Pretended it was all part the master plan.

Finally got noticed. Talent scout spots Animal. Then I never had to worry again, every nick I went they looked up my record put me straight in the squad.

Was up Norwich that first time, got there off some rave round Mildenhall where Jimmy Foley and me retailed a few things they never saw up Suffolk before. Got up Norwich found they played the cup final down Carrow Road, special day out for the cons, tea in the Executive Suite get your name Radio Broadland. Reckoned I could handle some of that. Chopped everyone all round the gym, got noticed, Class-A Animal.

Chief screw the football team was Mr Norton. Naughty to his friends although I never met one, Dickhead his enemies. Loved his football that Mr Norton, spot a ball artist a mile off, sodded them straight off the park. 'Wanker you're a fucking wanker!' he yelled, friendly like. 'Fuck off back your mother get me some psychos!'

Matter of fact there was some in the team could play for real only they were no use Mr Norton they weren't beasts in the bargain. Got to be choppers. Always easier playing against eight men than eleven he reckoned. Thin out the oppo early on. Only rule was no blade on the pitch could get us chucked out the league.

Loved his football that Mr Norton. Got his squad all sorted, slotted in his regular formation (one-nine-one we played or one-ten-one no one was counting) then someone got his release date coming up. Do his pieces.

'Fucking bastard!' he went demented he found out. 'Fucking cowardly lessie scumbag bastard!' Wanted you retaliating on him, assault on officer, Good Order And Discipline, down the block and lose ninety days only would you believe, you got let out the block play football. Best of all you took a machete on him and he maybe got you a whole new season. Told this eyetie winger his mum was a Protestant tart and got scabies, never reckoned the only English Nino knew was 'goal' and 'our ball' and 'fuck off you bleeder'. Got luckier on big John McCaw – called him a Celtic ponce, cracked three of Naughty's ribs. Naughty never minded, got big John for the play-offs.

Never got that cup final though. There was one team real hard men. Genuine article.

They heard about us and got prepared. Sorted us. Put two down the hospital, broken legs, not a bad result seeing hospital's an even better squeeze than football. Then one broken nose and one kidney failure three days later. We surrendered nine–two. Me I spent most the game behind the goal – sudden asthma attack. Like I say, never mix real hard geezers, they aren't impressed.

Chapter Six

We had a conference, me and The Mouth.

The Mouth had an office like the Beverly Hills attorney. On the street the paint peeled, yellow and white like an ice cream van and a big sign Flowerdew & Co knocked up by some chippie instead of readies. Never knew who the Co was, firm was Flowerdew and his runner. Inside was three secretaries, battery hens chained to the desks and squawking at Roy. Back in an office sat one woman lawyer no one ever heard of, maybe did the shady property deals. Then half-way down the corridor was young Norman, covered all the court Roy never fancied. Down the end was Roy. Paint peeled all the way. Then inside sudden fuck me it was Mr Big.

Office was the size of a runway and desk like a shithouse. Plants, carpet, everything shiny, even Roy and the carpet. Give you a Scotch you meant big readies, give you over young Norman you never. And Roy never refused you paid cash.

It was a conference. Normally only the wigs got

conferences only Roy, he had conferences.

'Nicky!' he cries, hand stretched.

'Roy!' I goes.

'Nicky!'

Could go on all night like this so I parked. Never fancied Scotch and he never rated Pernod suitable an attorney so I passed.

'Nicky, I've been looking at your statement right.' Time was money and Roy never wasted.

'Right.'

'You were there right.'

'Right.'

'But you haven't been charged with anything.'

'Why I got you Roy, make sure I ain't charged. Anyway I ain't done nothing and even I did you got to be able square it right?'

'I'm not sure what you mean by square it Nicky, but we'll work on the assumption that you ain't done nothing.'

'I ain't!'

'So where do I fit in?'

'You let on I ain't done nothing Roy.'

So he had a problem. Problem was you don't get legal aid when you never did anything and they never charge you. And no legal aid meant no readies for Roy. Got to keep him sweet.

'But I aim on doing something soon Roy, you could start lining it up like, use all this background work.'

'What do you plan on doing? As your lawyer I must advise you that I cannot be party to any conspiracy. Is it a big job?'

'Depends you call big. I reckon on plunging the geezer did Vinnie.'

'As your lawyer Nicky, I must advise you against murdering people.'

'This'll be manslaughter Roy. Unpremeditated.'

'I must advise you against unpremeditated man-slaughter also. Do you know who it's likely to be?'

'I got feelers.'

'In what direction?'

'Roy you wouldn't be minded on grassing me up would you?' Maybe he made a few that way too.

Roy leaned back in his chair. Been there near on ten years and still forgot his chair never tipped. They reckoned his missis made him get the hard chair for his back. So he reached for the cigs till he remembered she put a stop to them too.

'Nicky,' he goes, 'I think you're in serious water here.'

'I got to do it Roy,' I goes. 'Got to do it for Vinnie.'

'Vinnie's dead Nicky. Vinnie's brown bread, croaked, Vinnie's history. Nothing you can do'll bring him back.'

'Make me feel a lot better though. Got to do it Roy. Anyhow these geezers are on my case already so I just got to get in first or I'm wasted.'

'They'll more likely be after you if you start plunging people Nicky. Think on that my friend, they might give you a miss if you keep your head down.'

'Not them ones Roy.'

He fiddled with his tie, given out this year's advice.

'Where you staying Nicky?'

'Can't turn round and tell you Roy. No one reckons, not even me mum.'

'What about that bird of yours up Sycamore Court, that Kelly?'

'You got to be joking.'

'Or that Tina you used to know?'

'Do me a favour Roy.' I promised Marigold no one got
to know so I kept it. Roy Flowerdew never had the world's
smallest gob, employed him to open it not shut it.

'All right then. You keep in touch on the mobile and
you look after yourself, hear?'

'Got you.' I left the runway and went down the stairs
on Hoe Sreet. Walked up the market get a cab down the
Court. Reckoned I'd look in see Mum and Sharon and
Shithead and get some tea. Something The Mouth said
bothered me and I never even knew what it was yet, just
a rumble waiting for the big spew later on. First I needed
a think about it.

Priory Court was much the same since yesterday, they
still never laid the red carpet. Mum still never got the
dosh get her glasses mended, Sharon still feeding the kid
and Shithead still watching the news. I fetched a can off
Asif down the shop then went up. So the noise started.

'Nicky where you been?'

''Ullo Nicky,' goes Sharon.

'Grunt,' goes Shithead.

Sharon's kid jumps up and down, pleased to see me,
bangs his spoon.

So I sits down and Mum puts on another tin of beans
and makes some toast and I gives them the history. Some
of it. Like what they needed to know.

So I told them they never saw me and like as not they
never even heard of me. Told them I was with Ronnie
Good when he decked the geezers then Jimmy Foley

when he got blasted and now I was working on the answer only I didn't want to get plugged meantime so I was hid up. Never told them I planned on murdering anyone, thought it might cause a fuss. Told them I was well hid like, out the borough.

'Oh Nicky,' Mum turns round and says, 'didn't you ought to go up the Filth? Protection type of thing?'

No one else went anything. Too stupid for words really. First off the Bill never gave a toss on my account unless there was something I got they wanted. Second, even they did, what could they do? Fucking DS Grant wipe my arse every night? Change of identity? Hah bleeding hah. Last geezer I knew got police change of identity they moved him all the way up Chigwell, got sliced up first time he went down West Ham, half bleeding east London saw him sitting up the 58 bus.

So we all sat down watched the TV half an hour and I ate some beans then fucked off out. Went out the way I came in, over the wall and up Winns Avenue. Took a Sierra get up Chingford Hall. Never did know why anyone near Priory Court got a Sierra, all very well for your rep only you never had it available to drive around in. Average lifespan a Sierra on the Court was maybe twenty minutes. Put it in your bedroom might be safe otherwise forget it.

Had a choice of five Sierras on Winns Avenue, Sierra country round there, all scaffolders got mortgages. Getting dark it was so took a royal blue no problems, just off the main street. Never needed a motor getting over Chingford Hall in fact quicker walking only I might want it after so I reckoned get it now while I was in Sierra country.

Parked and went up the estate to see Chantel Living-stone, get more information, part of the master plan being hatched. First off I stopped off to see Runway Ricky, clock the tower was clear. While I was there reckoned I could get the news off him too.

Ricky put his eye to the hole, let me in.

'Nicky.'

'My man.'

'What can I do for you Nicky, you sniffing my sis again? Come in man, no harm trying.' He gave it teeth.

'Noreen in then?'

'Yeah she in. Come in Nicky man, want a rum and Coke?'

'Yeah.'

'Go in the kitchen man, they watching a video in here, I bring the stuff.'

'Hi Nicky,' his mum and dad called out from the front room, dark with the video on.

I went in the kitchen. Jesus that Noreen was in there getting a sandwich. Never been alone with her before. She turned round and smiled and went 'All right Nicky?' and smelled very sexy.

'Jesus you got good teeth Noreen,' I went. Stupid thing to say only she made me nervous, could hear my knees shaking.

'Comes of going to the dentist Nicky. How you been then?'

'You going out Noreen?'

'Yeah, I reckon do a bit of quiet raving eh?'

'You want to come out with me I got a motor downstairs.'

She laughed. I could see her tongue. I had to sit down.

'Nicky,' she went, 'you buy that motor or borrow it?'

'Borrowed it Noreen.'

'You going to take it back again?'

'Well . . . maybe now you mention it, maybe I will. Good idea, never thought of that. So where we going then like, I buy one straight after?'

She sat down the table near me, leaned over and I could clock down her tits only I never dared. 'Nicky,' she went careful, 'I believe I may have mentioned before' – she held up a minute – 'that I don't go out with people who thieve. Or murderers for that matter or rapists or . . .' she reckoned a bit, 'arsonists or drug addicts or hit men or dangerous drivers. You get the picture?'

'Fuck's sake Noreen,' I went, 'can't be many left.'

'One or two Nicky, be surprised. Only just at the minute you don't quite fit in the frame, do you?'

'I ain't no arsonist Noreen.'

'Well that's one out I suppose. The general idea is, though, I don't make it with criminals, you understand. Nor people might get rubbed out next week on some stupid war. You with me?'

'With you,' I went.

'So the choice got to be yours Nicky, eh. Give up the game, who knows, you might even get me.'

I considered it. 'Lot to ask Noreen,' I went.

'Well thank you very much mister.'

'No no,' I went hasty, 'do anything for you Noreen, you know that only . . .'

Then shit, in came Ricky carrying a tray and glasses and rum and Coke and ice. 'So how you two getting it on then eh?' he went.

Couldn't carry on then only not sure I wanted to or not. Broke the strain anyway. So I sat there watched that Noreen moving round the kitchen washing up her plate and things, see her bits moving this way and that way, then she wiggled her fingers at me and went out the door. Bathroom, probably the shower. Probably taking her bra off.

'Jesus Ricky,' I went, 'she some bird your sister or what?'

He laughed. 'Or what Nicky,' he went. Then he poured the drinks. Then I calmed down gradual, started the rum, felt it move round. Some time felt like a year later I felt cool again, remembered what I came up there for.

'Them geezers Ricky,' I went. 'You seen any of them geezers?'

'What geezers Nicky? Geezers done Vinnie?'

'Them geezers.'

Ricky sipped his glass, took time thinking. Then he sipped his glass again. Then he went 'You reckon I told you them geezers are serious Nicky. You could get dead just like that.'

I sipped and waited.

'I suggest you lay off, maybe take a vacation Nicky. You're my mate, you want Noreen get you a cheap fly somewhere, standby something?'

'Them geezers been around?' I went. 'Never go back next door only you clocked them round the estate?'

'Don't want you get hurt Nicky. One of them been seen on Sycamore Court.'

'Thanks Ricky.'

'You know they could come after me and my mum and dad Nicky, on account of I told you?'

'Yeah I reckon. Thanks Ricky. They won't hear.'

'They could do. Nothing you could do they seen you come up here.'

We sipped the rum, warm and clean. Yakked, watched

a bit of video, listened some sounds. Then I reckoned time to be further on. 'Tell you what Ricky,' I goes, 'how about I stay out the block until this is finished?'

'Be a favour Nicky. Not me you understand only Mum and Dad.'

I grabbed him thanks. Never even saw that Noreen gone out now, only thought about her in their shower about a year or two. Then went downstairs after that Chantel Livingstone, not such a pleasant experience.

Old Bill wasn't outside Ricky's now and no one around. Went down Chantel's and banged on her door. Luck would have it she was in and answered the door. Not so lucky, she was zonked. Speech blurred, eyes wide, pupils wide, feet slow.

'Hey Nicky,' she goes, slurry. I went in.

'Chantel.'

'Nicky. Want a cup of coffee and that?'

'No thanks. You all right Chantel?'

'Never felt better.' She was dribbling a bit.

Best time to lean on scag habits was when they wanted it or when they were too far to care. She was a long way.

'Chantel where you find the man these days?'

'Find the man? Don't know what you mean Nicky.' They all lied when they used gear.

'You get your stuff off Andrew Okema like you said?'

Upped her bonce. 'How'd you know?'

'You reckoned last time it was the African. Still covers the estate eh?'

'He might do . . .' She was leaning back on her settee falling asleep, skirt up round her fanny. 'Might do . . .'

'Where's his base now Chantel? Left here, got to have a base, or is he mobile?'

'Got to have a base . . .'

Fuck me, I could even feel sorry for the pigs they had to deal with this. 'Where's his base Chantel?'

'Where's his base . . . who?'

'Andrew Okema. He got a place on Sycamore now?'

'Sycamore.' It woke her up a bit. 'How'd you know, Nicky? Yeah, Sycamore.' She went to sleep a minute, woke up again. 'You want a bit of gear off him Nicky? Comes here every day you know . . .'

So she reckoned it was Sycamore only Andrew never wanted her round there so he made house calls. Wouldn't get more off Chantel anyway on account of she was snoring. Next stop had to be Kelly.

Shut Chantel's door, went down the stairs and out the car park. No one I could clock. Had to keep roads clear on account of not wanting Ricky Hurlock shot up, then again never wanted getting shot up my own account. Went on a detour round the front the estate and up Hazel Way. Back slid in Sycamore not making a broadcast. Up the stairs heart banging like shit, got to Kelly's and hammered on the door.

No answer. Hammered on the door again. This time the evening no way she wasn't there. Hammered again. Not the Old Bill knock just a hammer.

She came to the door, looked through the hole.

'Who is it?' she went.

'Me course you jerk-off, you fucking know who it is.'

'He ain't in.'

Pardon? He ain't in? Who ain't in? Brain cells may be not so young any more but what the fuck was she going on about?

'What you say?'

'He ain't in.'

'No he ain't in he's bleedin' standing here. Let me the fuck in Kelly, I got to talk with you.'

'He ain't in. Sod off or I . . .'

'You . . .' Then sudden the door burst open and this big shiny black guy stood rippling. Very big. Pointed his finger at me. Good enough for me, very convincing.

'She say he ain't in, got that?'

'Got it. He ain't in I reckon. Sorry to disturb you geezer. I'll come back another time.'

'Do that. Or don't do that. You got that too?'

Fuck.

It had to be Andrew Okema. Didn't have to ask see his birth certificate. No one else that mean around, least no one else African and that mean and on Sycamore Court.

I had the choice, chuck him out the window on account of he was putting it up Kelly and got my kid in there, or find the exit.

I already knew where the exit was.

Shit and fuck. Explained a lot, like why Kelly was awkward last time around. I was certain Ricky never knew or he never sent me there, but there were other questions. Was the gear there last time around? Did the pigs know Andrew was around?

Then again there was something The Mouth said worried me.

Kelly and Andrew Okema. Fuck me.

Wandsworth

Matter of fact, soon after sentence I got a Dear John off that Kelly. On account of everything happened perhaps, or maybe she just never loved me any more. Quite amusing as it turned out. Up to now I've got thirteen Dear Johns off that Kelly. Due another in the mail. Still coming up on visits, brings the kid, just goes home and sends a Dear John after.

First one even wasn't all bad, brought my introduction to the welfare and his problems. There I was, straight after sentence, before the tour of the country, the welfare sent for me said he wanted to discuss problems.

Two days after reception I was counting on a bit of a breather. Later on maybe staring at the walls listening to the sob spots on Capital Gold you could handle getting out the cell, only first two days you get called up everyone bar the milkman. Called by the MO points his stethoscope at you, reckons you're A1 except you got a personality disorder. Called up all three chaplains (try out all the churches like, sort of test drive). Called up the governor or dep, tells you you're in prison, case you never noticed. Reckoned I'd just take in the library then have a little lie-down when I got the call the welfare wanted a rap about problems.

Some nicks the welfare comes and gets you, this one the screws took you. So there I was delivered personal by my escort once he felt like it, and there it was on the door, Mr J McIver Probation Officer.

'Mr Burkett!' he cried. 'Good to see you!' he cried. Like he never just called me up and we'd never clapped on each other before, more like we fixed a meeting down the boozer after a blagging. He had a beard, like they do.

'Mr Burkett,' he went on, 'come in please, make yourself comfortable, take a seat. Thank you Mr Forrest,' to the screw. 'My name's Jim McIver, I'm a probation officer down here you know, like the welfare, and I cover your wing. We have this arrangement with the prison officers that they deal with all routine matters but we take over for all of what you might call special problems, you know?' he went hopefully.

'Yes Mr McVicar,' I went.

'Er yes. Well Mr Burkett, I'll get straight to the point shall I, would you like a cup of tea?'

'Yes please Mr McVicar.' Never let them even get started they don't produce the rosie. Always got a kettle stashed somewhere. Next stop was a fag only you got to have those special problems for that.

He made with the kettle.

'Mr Burkett, Nicholas . . . As you know I expect, we see everyone soon after sentence to see if there is anything we can help with and to help draw up your sentence plan. Meanwhile though I felt I should call you up straight away because I wondered if there were, you know, any extra problems for you at present?'

'Sentence is a bit of a problem Mr McVicar,' I went. 'You can't do nothing about that eh?'

'Er no, I'm afraid that's one for your lawyers Mr Burkett. Nick.'

He dunked the tea bag. Never looked a promising cup of tea. Say what you like about the women welfare, they definitely made a better brew.

'Now then er Nick, I believe you had a Dear John this morning.'

'Oh that Mr McVicar.' So that was the knockings. They reckoned somewhere some European court made it illegal reading prisoners' mail. Tell that the British nicks. Hah bleeding hah. Censor been busy again, never noticed he didn't exist. 'Oh that,' I laughed.

'This was from your er partner Nick?'

'My name's Nicky, Mr McVicar.'

'I was very sorry to hear that Nicky and of course I do realise that I shouldn't get to hear about it through prison censorship which I assure you I disapprove of – nevertheless I am aware that you must be experiencing deep pain at present, with this following on from your heavy sentence, and I just thought you might wish to talk about your feelings in a safe environment.'

'You got a fag Mr McVicar?' Deep pain had to be at least a cig.

He got them out a drawer and some matches. Knew they had to be somewhere. Poor old welfare he coughed and spluttered and opened the windows, never smoked himself only believed freedom of choice so he said. Me I felt a good bit better.

'Oh that Mr McVicar,' I carried on now. 'That was only that Kelly. Last sentence I got five Dear Johns off five different birds would you believe, there was slags all over London went they never wanted to see me no more. Always more birds though Mr McVicar, eh? That

Kelly, take her a night out up the Stow, couple of vodkas, soon be on her back Mr McVicar.' Went for that talk the welfare, always fancied a bit of rough.

'I see,' he went. 'I see.' Stroked his beard a bit. 'Now you and Kelly Nicky, do you have any children?'

'Who me?' I went. Always went 'who me?' on every-one in nick like there was six of us. Lost their cool.

'Yes you.'

'Oh me.'

'Do you and Kelly have any children?'

'Yeah.'

'Many?'

'No Mr McVicar, not many.'

'Er how many?'

'Let me see, one I reckon.'

'Is that a boy or a girl Nicky?'

'Yeah.'

'Er which is it Nicky?'

'It's a boy course.'

'A boy, that's nice. I must show you the photographs of my children. What's his name?'

'Danny.'

'Do you think Kelly will bring Danny up to visit you in spite of this, or perhaps she might arrange for someone else to bring him up? Or we can always arrange special visits you know. Have you had family problems in the past? I see from reports that your mother and father separated when you were very young.'

Now we were talking. Bleeding hard work getting him round but now he was making right noises. Special visits was top result, bit of smoke, sometimes a cubicle so you even got a hand job, beat the workshop any day. 'Yeah Mr McVicar,' I went enthusiastic, 'now you come to mention it I reckon a few special visits might help to mend our relationship and definite give an assist to that rehabilitation.'

As it happened, second special visit alarms went and would you believe they forgot us five minutes and I put it in her behind the door! No one ever credited it, all the cons reckoned impossible on special visits only it happened. Kelly and me don't know which one was giggling most after. Definite helped my rehabilitation and probably remorse as well. It was wicked.

So it does no harm you keep up connections on the welfare. No call to get friendly or you get the psycho treatment, only cups and fags and sometimes a special can't be bad. Even a draft comes up sudden you reckon you can't possibly transfer on account of you're in the middle very important therapy with the welfare, vital to your sentence plan. Most likely they blow that before breakfast, rate the welfare somewhere under rabies on the health scale, only worth a try you're desperate. Only never bother family connections though, they never give a toss your crippled grannie can't get her wheelie up Durham.

So then I went off on the country tour. Got back and would you believe the welfare was still there, reckoned I got more problems!

♦

I was just getting round to putting in the app for a fag and special visit when the welfare called me up first. So excited could hardly wait on the screw getting out the door.

'Nicky!' he cried.

'Mr McVicar!' I went.

'Please call me Jim. Nicky, I have been looking at your prison file and I do believe you take a French newspaper!'

'That's right Mr McVicar.' Not even any tea yet let alone a smoke.

'You mean to say you can read French?'

'Course I can. Bit of trouble with English sometimes mind.'

'Well!' Really set him off, seemed like all my problems ten times bigger now I could read French. Could see his beard curling.

'You really can read French?' he went again.

'Fuck me Mr McVicar course I can read bleedin' Froggie, don't think I'd waste my spends else do you?' Matter of fact I always took *L'Équipe* when I was inside. Came expensive but worth it you wanted solid reading. Get through the library James Clavell and Wilbur Smith and G F Newman then you wanted a paper lasted more than five minutes, so I got *L'Équipe*. Had all English football and more besides. No one took the piss, anyway I couldn't give a fuck. Better than clocking the walls.

'But Nicky,' went the welfare, happy as shit, 'it says on the files as well that you are dyslexic!'

'That's right Mr McVicar. Vegetarian an' all. Says so on all the forms innit? Vegetarian and dyslexic. Veggie and dizzie. Only dyslexic in English though, not Froggie.'

Veggie and dizzie. I always went veggie and dizzie on reception every nick, saved a lot of aggravation. Vegetarian you never had to eat shit. Vegan could be even better only some nicks you never got anything aside from beans. Dizzie you never had to do anything you didn't fancy, just fucked up and they let you back on the wing some kind of nutter. Even you got nicked somewhere you had no business just went you couldn't read the notice. Almost on the scale chapel orderly got God on your side. Epileptic could be handy too, anyone got on your case you just had a fit only I never tried that yet. Allergies were getting popular as well.

'You're really vegetarian and dyslexic Nicky?'

'Course.'

'And you read French and you've got family problems!' I never had to ask for the tea and a fag, he got them right out there and then.

'Where did you learn French Nicky?'

'School Mr McVicar.'

'And have you ever been to France?'

'Matter of fact I do go Calais fence some gear once in a while. Otherwise I sooner go up Canvey you know.'

Didn't want to know about the gear or probably Canvey so he got busy with the kettle. 'And does your mother read French too Nicky?' he went sudden.

Had to be a bit careful here. Next stop it was Mum and Stepdad and my life of crime. Read about it in my court report. Read about it in Simenon as well. Put him off the track I reckoned.

'No my mum's Irish Mr McVicar,' I went.

He really dunked that tea bag then. We sat down for a long cool smoke. He damn near had one himself even.

'Nicky,' he goes, 'did you ever think of writing all this down? Like I mean it's all sitting there in your head – a great big family saga, a history of cause and events – and it might help you to make sense of it all if you saw it written down in front of you.'

'Only I'm dyslexic Mr McVicar,' I went. 'And vege-tarian.'

'Well I'm sure we could help you with that. It could be a real chance for you.'

'And the chaplain already suggested it like.'

'Ah. He suggested what exactly?'

'Like writing it down, a few sins. Only I told him he couldn't beady it Mr McVicar and nor could you cause that wouldn't be straight now would it? You beadying it and not him?'

'No . . . no, that's right. But what do you think about it Nicky?'

'I'll give it consideration Mr McVicar,' I went, leaned back and sipped the Rosie. 'I'll give it every consideration.'

Wasn't that bad the welfare. Never let him put his eye on a fucking word though. He clocked that and I never got back in the cell.

Chapter Seven

We met down the Standard Rameez and me, discuss tactics hands-on style. There was Rameez and his posse, me on my tod. Have to learn, gangster meetings you took your counsellor and a few muscles.

Was heavy rock night but hard to tell the difference down the Standard. Could tell it wasn't ballet classes. Heavy dudes, big jackets and big women. Voices sounded same as their engines. Bump their elbows you got the iron necklace. I kept out the Standard heavy rock nights or even most other nights, never had the manners for it.

Heavy rock meant about as much to Rameez like marine biology. Was on his manor though so he reckoned he ought to take an interest, show his face. Not for me to argue he wanted a meeting there.

Got there early, grabbed a table before they all got turned over. Had a lager before Rameez arrived. Got in the corner, made sure I never glanced even five metres near some bird else her grizzly took a spanner to me. Kept my Judge Dread down round my toes twenty minutes.

Then Rameez made his entrance.

Swept in like he parked the Lotus outside. White jacket, shiny black shoes. Knew he toddled up from home, Coppermill Lane, so did Kevin the gaffer. Grizzlies didn't though, only knew Rameez was the article round there.

'All right Rameez,' went Kevin off the bar.

'All right Kev mate.' Rameez and the posse got their Pernods, clocked me and came over.

'Nicky.'

'Rameez.'

'How's business Nicky?'

'Mustn't grumble Rameez. Yourself? Heard you lifted good gear down the trading estate last night, quality goods I heard.'

'You ain't wired Nicky I suppose?'

I laughed. 'No I ain't. Want a look?' Was just paying him a compliment like I heard he got class electronics out a warehouse.

Blonde piece walked in the door, not Walthamstow or I'd known her. Looked like problems on someone's bill, expensive. Saw Rameez, came over. Not the one wagging her tits at him up Tottenham. The posse got her a chair off one side, he put a mitt on her shoulder let the grizzlies deck she was his, then came back for the business. Bought me a Pernod – gesture of good faith, never mind I wanted a lager.

'So what the crack Nicky?'

'You in Rameez?'

'I might be in Nicky. Only you never forget there's readies in it do you?'

'I never forget Rameez. Setting up a deal.'

'And you give me the deal when we settle the rest eh?'

Seemed to be like how it was done then. Bit of a relief when I never dreamed up the deal yet.

'Give you the works Rameez, when I set it up. Never insult you on a half job, you reckon that. Get it sorted first.'

'Good thinking Nicky. Get the whole bit of work. Now brief me the history, eh.'

Gave him the history. Names he already knew and what happened Vinnie. Told him Tina and Sherry and then Ronnie Good down the Flowerpot. Told him Jimmy Foley and how I was hid up. Told him Chantel, left out Ricky Hurlock. Told him Andrew Okema was on Sycamore, confirmed I clocked him there myself.

'Where he hang out?'

'Got a flat they say, empty or a sub.'

'That where you seen him?'

'No.'

'Where you seen him?'

'Up my bird's.'

Rameez put his glass down. Whistled. 'Up your bird's Nicky?'

'Last night. Never knew when I seen you Sunday.'

'You got your honour to straighten Nicky. Like they both must die.'

'Yeah maybe.' More concerned I had a bed to stay up Kelly's on late nights only did no harm Rameez reckoned it my honour as well as his. Needed him to know it serious too though, not just some tart. 'And honour for my mate,' I went.

'Yeah.'

We gave a decent pause.

'So what we got Nicky? Three very mean men, cars

and shooters, deals Class-A drugs and brings protection out Canning Town, serious attitude geezers.'

'I heard you was mean too, Rameez.'

'Not that mean Nicky. We got to have a campaign, we got to get them when they aren't aware, we got to balance the odds. How we going to do all that?'

'There's a big stash of powder Rameez. Reckon it could get some assist?'

'Not so sure I want that assist Nicky. You know my religion would prevent me making deals with Class-A geezers.' Rameez got his pills up Tottenham was sipping his Pernod only he got very religious round powder.

My turn to buy the Pernods so Rameez sent one of the minders up the bar, Pernods all round. My dosh. Big geezer – Aftab Malik. Aftab was just coming back with a trayful when sudden war broke out.

It gave us some of the answers, me and Rameez.

Geezer named Mervyn was bopping to the sounds. Very big geezer, made Aftab look midgy, very big black jacket, very small brain. Kind of fixture down the Standard, heavy rocker, never had a bike only wore the gear. Mixed with the bikers, humoured him. Shame about the brain, his mum was all right ran a stall on the market, Mervyn worked there Saturdays frightened off the customers.

Then some feller out of town, like Epping, wore a suit would you believe, probably a car dealer, reckoned Mervyn was in his space.

Feller had his mates there too. All told Mervyn where he ought to be standing. Tried to establish respect.

You had to speak gentle to Mervyn. No problem at all you speak gentle to him. Only he never liked it you told him where to stand when he was bopping the sounds.

Picked up the geezer from Epping, threw him over two

tables, landed on my Pernods Aftab was carrying. Broke all the glasses.

Aftab reckoned this was bad manners, upsetting a geezer's Pernod, and I was their guest in the bargain. Was forced to use the glass slice the feller's cheek. Knew Rameez never liked bad manners.

Meanwhile the rest of Epping joined in on Mervyn. Mervyn never needed a lot of assist only Walthamstow lent a hand just in case. Couple of bottles, few wrenches. Me I never made out how they kept wrenches comfortable in their pockets while they were bopping but they seemed they always wanted them available. Certain came in handy now.

All over a few moments. Before the Bill arrived me and Rameez slid out the road, have a quiet drink up the Palmerston.

'Really sorry Nicky,' goes Rameez up the Palmerston. 'Really really bad manners invite you then something like that happen. Your drink got spilled as well.'

'Mention it Rameez, not your fault geezer. Feller stepped out of line, Mervyn got to do what he did. Then Aftab was unfortunate got in the way. No worries. Got to teach a lesson.'

'Appreciate it Nicky.'

We sipped the drinks he bought, me on lager now and him gin and lime, reckoned he liked the colour.

'You reckon we could get them geezers in a ruck like that?' he went sudden.

I stared at him. Could see where he was leading. 'Can see where you're leading Rameez,' I went. 'Jesus Rameez.'

'See what I'm thinking?'

'See what you're thinking.'

'How do we get them there Nicky? Them's very big geezers.'

'Never come.'

'How do we get them there? We got some chance a place like that. No chance we get in some shoot-out. Fuck me.'

'Fuck me Rameez.' My poor little brain was ticking. 'Fuck me Rameez.'

'How the fuck we get them to a gig Nicky?'

'We got to get them to a gig Rameez. We got to get them all there, no use one or two. We got to have some reason they want to go there.'

We thought about that.

'Only one reason they come Nicky,' went Rameez, 'they want to kill us.'

We thought about that too.

'True words,' I went.

We were agreed.

♦

'Where we going to aim at Nicky?' went Rameez. It was next night only this time we went down The Village. Not likely spot really yakking on gang warfare, mostly teachers and computer programmers, if they heard us probably reckoned we were on about some film we just saw. Only me and Rameez this time round, reckoned we'd get somewhere quiet, no interruptions.

We both had some thoughts overnight. No doubt it had to be a gig. Lot of heads in there, no one reckoned what was going down. Murder a few geezers and bit of luck no one noticed.

'It got to be a gig,' I went.

'Where we going to aim at Nicky?' went Rameez.

'Got to be a big event. Got to be a wedding or a charity. What I whistle up Brian Dear lay on a wedding?'

'Reckon not Nicky. Weddings is sacred.'

Forgot Rameez was religious.

'Charity then. Got to be a big one. We want a venue and we want a charity Rameez.'

'Venue. You got ideas?'

'Assembly Rooms is biggest. Mostly Jewish there. Jewish anniversary something?'

'You Jewish Nicky?'

'Could be.'

'Could be fuck. They never let you have it you not smart enough. Where else?'

'Asian Centre?'

He sat back.

'Jesus Nicky, why I never thought of that? Just over the road here.'

'Could be best place Rameez?'

'Jesus. Bit small maybe but we could fill it. Charity get the elders and the churches. Mosque, temple, gurdwara, even Christians, never know. Fire regulations maybe four hundred so we squeeze in a thousand. Jesus Nicky.'

Charity gigs were the top. Get the churches and you were made up. Some crippled blue-eyed girl needed an op California some place, you got the whole borough out. Charge a fiver take a quid commission and half the bar profits you never worried on the bus fare home. Not to mention drug profits off the Es. Get the venue for free probably and disco for expenses keep all the overheads down. Still at school we used to do it, three of us cleared seven hundred sobs one Saturday down

McEntee. Proper excellent, got drunk a week all through classes.

'Jesus Rameez fuck me man. You reckon you can get the Asian Centre?'

'Got to ask. No chance this weekend, see if it free next week. Gets booked up. Maybe lean on someone postpone a booking.'

'Postpone their wedding Rameez?'

He grinned. 'You taking the piss Nicky?'

We thought some more. 'OK Rameez like say we book the place get a thousand in. Want Micky and Errol and Andrew know we there. Now why they come?'

He had it sorted.

'One,' he goes, 'you do something make them plenty mean. Plenty mean I'm telling you. Two, you let them know you're taking over their op. Three, you let them know we're running the gig and we dealing there.'

It could work.

Only there were gaps, like how anyone take us serious and how we got them plenty mean.

'How is it we get them plenty mean?' I went.

He had this sorted too. 'You shoot one,' he went.

When I finished coughing down my beer asked him to repeat himself.

'You shoot one,' he went. 'Not fatal just damage. Then you tell him you're taking over and the rest.'

'Thought you were the warrior Rameez? How the fuck you think I'm going to shoot someone?'

'With a gun Nicky. You forget you just hire me and my friends for the finale. You set it up before with sharp planning.'

'Oh.'

'Then when you tell him you're taking over, we put

the word round every druggie in the area there's a big sale down the Asian Centre the gig Saturday or whenever. First off, everyone reckons we took over the op, no other way getting the powder. Second, it's like we just put a rod up their arses. They got to come Nicky.'

I whistled. 'You been thinking heavy Rameez. I'm supposed to be planning but you been thinking heavy for me.'

'I been thinking heavy Nicky. You just got to shoot the guy and then some other way you just get all the loot to recompense me and my friends.'

'Yeah. Get all the dosh.'

We had a few more. We got up walked round separate, came back both giggling. It was brilliant. I knew Rameez would go for it if he thought up the rap. Saved me doing the thinking in the bargain. It was brilliant.

'Fuck me man,' he went. 'It just brilliant. Only tell me Nicky, what the fuck my mum and dad going to tell my grandparents I get sliced? I got one lot of grandparents over here got some idea but the others back in Lahore. What the fuck they going to tell them I got murdered in gang war? Bring shame on the family man.'

'Tell them you were upholding Walthamstow honour.'

'Then what about my marriage prospects? Not only a murdered gangster but got a scar all down one side?'

He laughed. Me I reckoned it was a bit late thinking about his grandparents now. Two thousand crimes back he could have given it a moment.

'You're a gangster already Rameez,' I went. 'Only so far you're a small gangster. Now you got opportunity being a big one. Real like villain.'

'And all because you ask me on account of my honour Nicky. Must book me for crazy eh?'

'Wouldn't ask you I didn't book you for crazy.'

He laughed and I got him his next gin and lime.

'So how much your fee Rameez?' I went.

'Five K.'

'Five K?'

'Five K.'

Make me look weak I argued. Thought out the sums. First find out a charity only maybe leave that for Rameez, got the connections. Book the hall must be some dosh, even overheads. Asian Centre never make much on the drinks even you bring them yourself. Your mates do the door for you. Asian Centre bound to have a licence so don't have to apply the music. Get the sounds probably cheap. Tickets got to be printed and there was advertising. Five pounds a ticket, got to give over four pounds the charity and they probably got someone looking. Be lucky I cleared a half thou. Then Rameez wanted five K. He never knew I didn't get the work lined up yet for paying him.

I got to go to work.

Bought Rameez another few, he bought another few. Too drunk either of us lift a motor so we got a cab. Dropped him Coppermill Lane then I carried on up Stoke Newington. Not too drunk to be careful so he dropped me up Dalston and I got another cab back Marigold's. She was asleep, left some beans in the pan.

Wandsworth

Old days they used to lift TVs. Hard to imagine, in the back window, put some forty-two-inch over your shoulder and out again down the market. Got to be Superman make any lettuce. TVs never fitted in a paper bag so you had to look a right paddy trotting down the High Street one on each shoulder. But it was TVs the punters wanted, so it was TVs you half-inched. These days everyone got four in their bedroom you never give one away, those days some never even got colour. Supply and demand.

Then there was LPs the same. Tell me LPs were the monte, never get enough the second-hand shops and markets. Sounds a doss nicking LPs, only you ever tried catching a bus three dozen LPs in your bag? Then maybe some student you just lifted them off comes home early chases you up the road? Young and fit got to be students. Leave it out.

Easy enough retail them only hard bleeding graft doing the work. Thank God modern inventions. I got a job once brickie's labourer carrying hods up and down ladders, not half as hard running up High Street two carriers of LPs under your arm.

The job went the same way as LPs. So you got to look at sources of income.

Little while cassettes seemed like the answer, came

along nice and light only never worth the aggravation, everyone got a pocketful and cassettes are crap. As it goes sounds went out the window all ways. Anyone got a stack buys the pirates, never knew anyone bought a cassette off a shop. Then CDs came along only never a market for them thieving, whoever bought them didn't live Walthamstow or least never lived Walthamstow and shopped round the second-hands and snooker halls.

Videos were good business a while. Anyone you know bought a new video? Course not, too dear. Everyone knew some geezer get one on the side. Bit dodgy in second-hands for a bit on account of they could check where it was new. Nowadays though no one gets fussed, everyone and the cat knows they're lifted. Once used they call it or once nicked. Buy one in a minicab you want.

Videos were good business, still not too bad. Got a video get it insured else the companies shaft you on the small print. Bought it in a minicab mind, tough shit on the insurance or get done receiving. Just reckon you lost it same way you got it and buy a burglar alarm.

Fact never fuss on the alarm only get the box goes on the wall says burglar alarm. Kid clocks it not going to try it find out it works. Visit your neighbour never got one instead.

Live up a block you got no cover. Never any alarms tower blocks anyway no one'd take notice. Flats too easy to get in and away and the people can hear are probably people broke in. Knew three kids once got a commission on a three-piece. Waited till the bird went upstairs after a cup of milk, lifted the whole suite before she got back. Anyway Old Bill never makes it up blocks, takes too long the nick up the eighteenth and then they reckon it's all villains up there, not worth the bother.

Word processors, VDU and that. Seemed like the article. Not long ago I lifted one out an estate agent on Hoe Street. Walked in took it no problem, no one seemed upset. Reckoned I was moving in the modern world, get in the technology. And worth half a motor. Only trouble was couldn't jingle it.

Can't take it down the market or up Wood Street antiques. Then again look a proper perve wander up some office block the city – er scuse me guv, you interested nice second-hand VDU for her indoors? Do me a favour. Then it's a bleeding great fucker too, nearly bust an arm walking home. In the bargain it never fit under my bed. So I finished up giving it away for a bunch, impossible get a fair price. Bad planning.

Not half as bad some cases though. Once got fourteen hundred dimmer switches only that's another story. My mate Sean Loveless finished up one time thirty boxes carbon paper and four hundred packets Weetabix. Then again there was Darren Boardman – called him the tote on account of he was an accumulator.

Fourteen years old, Darren got thirty-five TVs at home, up the stairs round the walls out on the balcony. Wandered round picked them where he found them, down the dump on a skip or out someone's front room he happened to look in. Loved his TVs Darren. Mum never got in his room. In the bargain was couple of dozen radios, few computers and a million fish. Burgled a house up Chingford only lifted the tropical fish, know what I mean? Two in the morning round his, Darren was there decking fourteen TV screens all different channels. Fuck knows where he got them, make anything work and it was stations all over Europe not just satellites and cable. Screens everywhere and fish all lit up in the dark. Weird.

Got nine months YOI one time Darren only they never wanted let him out. Kept all the TVs and videos going were on the blink and then their office computers, washing machines the lot. Happy as a pig in shit. Never did a sentence like normal, always drinking tea round some screw's house getting the video in order. Cost them a half-ounce instead of fifty sobs up the dealer's. Being Darren, never even reckoned his release date, quite happy up there long as his mum fed the fish. Only on visits we worked out the dates, wrote anonymous up the governor otherwise he was probably there still.

Anyway you got to move with the times you want to do a bit of work worth doing. Got to look up new material. Personal computers are business till everyone got one. Key finders are small change but sell one any pub in England. Car phones are serious dosh, forget the cassette there's a mobile there. They reckon laser printers never miss you've got an entry in the print.

Me I never made serious paper off motors. Never got the interest, never rode for cash. Either you rode for riding or you rode for retail, almost never knew geezers mixed it. Rode for retail and you meant quality motors, new Mercs and Jags and Porsches, pass them on within the hour, change the chassis number and on the road. Not many Porsches round Walthamstow for a start off. More likely it was Wayne Sapsford or Mercedes Marty Fisherman liked to have a ride round before bedtime. Marty only once ever got a Merc, never left off telling us though. Rode bleeding everything else as it goes. Cavaliers, Escorts, Astras, Golfs, not too fussy. Not so clever driving though, once nicked a left-hand-drive Renault, got confused went straight over a roundabout. Used to get itchy he never rode that day, reckoned he'd even ride a Fiesta. Saturday nights always got a Ford take-away then Chinese take-away.

One time he was in the Bay, Old Bill came up visiting Marty, went they did an amnesty, wanted to write off a million car jobs. Make their clear-up rate look good. First off Marty bottled out, reckoned it was throw away the key he held his hand up on all his motors. Then he got the chaplain witness they promised no charges. So he trilled like a canary, got some entertainment.

Chaplain reckoned it was like the Book of Psalms. Got the crime sheets out the briefcase – one sheet each TWOC. Happened I was visits orderly, nearly came in on witness myself. They got about three hundred sheets and Marty he claimed about a hundred and eighty.

They went 'Now Marty, this Civic on Shernhall, twenty-seventh October, you know about that one?' and he went 'Shernhall yeah just by Marlowe yeah I reckon I had a Civic there Mr Levy, wanted a new clutch.' Or 'No, Mr Golding, I never had anything away out the front McDonald's, too many buses in the way down there Mr Golding.' Went like that two hours, cleared up half the crime round Waltham Forest sitting up visits on the Bay. Marty wasn't too sure to trust the Bill only he never got charged.

Me I looked up other sources of income like I say. Softest I ever had was up west down Leicester Square. Simplest was breaking windows. Reckoned I might want some of that again now.

Lived up west a bit when I was sixteen, never had a place like only crashed a few clubs or Centrepoint occasional. Earn a few bob the clubs at that. You were black could get paid dancing start the evening, only white

kids never got the offer, couldn't move I reckon. Me I
earned on errands or watch the motors or guard on
the police after the pills. Then again clubs might want
you on the door someone never rolled in. Not official,
about a foot too short, sort of backup they put the boot
in. Bit brutal all that. Made the real dosh on the dog
and bones.

Heavy earner was that little scam. Down Leicester
Square you got bag bandits, score merchants the lot,
only who needed getting involved? Callboxes were
always there waiting.

Tourists always belled Germany every night. Never
knew the currency, reckoned it was cheap anyway. Put
say four quid in, made the call saw the money ticking
away. What they never knew was the cash never fell
down their way when they only used the half. Never
fell down on account of we stuck a card across there.
Least it fell down half-way then it got stuck.

Tourists reckoned they never understood the money
or else it was bleeding British machines again. Turned
round went out, just another rip-off. Me, I walked up took
ownership of a quid or two. Made profit round eighty to
a oner a day. Not so bad dosh a sixteen-year-old. Never
did fancy that begging.

Simplest bit of work though was definite breaking
windows. So easy-peasy it got embarrassing.

You run out of change Friday night down the boozer.
You walk down the High Street with a brick. Sling
it through the window any clothes shop, least any
geezers' clothes shop. Lift a few jackets, back in the
boozer and retail them. Carry on drinking. Few alarm
bells sound off, only there's about two old biddies and a
cat walking the High Street, Bill never take notice alarm

bells. Time it gets noisy after three or four is when you're somewhere else.

Want to get classy about it you best get in the back door only then you got to have tools. More likely get nicked walking innocent down the street with a few tools they reckon going equipped. Never heard anyone get nicked smashing windows. Get a bit more professional and you got a van waiting, lift couple hundred jackets and some shirts. Take them down the wholesaler's or maybe snooker halls. Never get full value mind only part of the game. Worth probably three thou, shop claims six off insurance and you get half a thou. Got to be realistic.

You got to stay with the game and you got to stay mobile, never get stuck one play. Now I wanted a very big payday and I wanted a very big assist. First I had to get the assist.

Chapter Eight

Jimmy Foley was sitting up wearing Whipps Cross pyjamas. Looked like normal, not very sharp. Tubes coming out most directions. Saturday two o'clock watching the racing. I spent three days hiding up and belling some assist. Reckoned now was the hour to visit up Jimmy.

'Jimmy,' I turns round and says 'you looking fierce man.'

'Fuck off,' he goes. 'Hey up Nicky, I got in the paper you take a butcher's? Victim of gang war. Only trouble was some war I never declared.'

'Brought you two hundred Benson's and a few cans,' I went.

'Sainsbury's?'

'Getting a rep down there. Went up Buy Best.'

'Thanks Nicky. Put 'em under the bed.'

'How you doin' Jimmy?'

'Rough. Be better after them cans. Got any weed? Quack reckons I'm one fuckin' lucky geezer.'

'His exact words?'

'Near as. Missed everything, went out the side. Fuckin' hurt Nicky. Now I'm bored as shit sat in here. Mum been every day. Few birds. Few mates, Brendan and Elvis and that. Nurses give me a feel now and again, slip in the bed at night.'

'Oh yeah? Jimmy I need your assist.'

'Last time I gave you my assist Nicky got plugged.'

'Chance to get it sorted. Pay them off for you.'

'Like a gunfight? Clear the market, shoot it out?'

Problem with Jimmy was on account of he wasn't Mr Einstein on the brains you never knew to laugh or not. Gave him the story instead. Told him the plan Rameez and me. Told him Rameez wanted five K upfront.

'Rameez?' he went. 'He still scare the shit out of you Nicky?'

'You reckon. Better he's with us Jimmy, him and his mates. Then again you know the schemes, reckon who got what bit of work. Guess you're involved. Give you commission course.'

'Tell you what Nicky.'

'What?'

'Social giros. I got angles on a stash. Like large. Never knew what the fuck I did with them.'

'Real?'

'Legit. Real article. Not even made out. Make them out who the fuck you like, how much you like.'

'Where you get them?'

'Exchange some pills.'

'Where you stash them?'

'Under the mattress.'

'Mattress! What fuckin' mattress?'

'What fuckin' mattress you think? One I'm lying on.'

'Jesus Jimmy.' They turned the fucking mattress about six times a day in there. I lifted the mattress. There was a packet of Social giros, Income Support cheques only all blank. Genuine kosher only no name or amount. Counted them. Two hundred.

'Fuckin' roll on Jimmy, who scanked them books?'

'Never matter. Geezer up the Social I reckon, came second-hand my way.'

'How you get them in here?'

'Were zipped in my jacket. They took it off on account of I got shot you remember. Never searched it.'

'What you want for them Jimmy?'

'Three parts payment Nicky.'

'Run it by me Jimmy.'

'One, you get the geezers plugged me.'

'Do our best. Stick by your mates.'

'Two, I get a grand.'

Jimmy not as dim I thought. 'Reckoned you were my mate Jimmy,' I went, protesting.

'Got me shot being your mate.'

'Bought you a Guinness first.'

'Fuck off Nicky.'

'OK. Only reasonable the circumstances. Compensation. We get paid, you get paid.'

'Three, you get me down West Ham three o'clock.'

'What? Today?'

'Now.'

I laughed. Couldn't help it. Me I got down West Ham occasional when the Scousers came for a bundle otherwise I never bothered. Jimmy went regular. Today it was Leeds. Jimmy got to be there, hated Leeds almost like Scousers.

'Jimmy give me the story on them Social giros,

like how you deal it man, then we get up West Ham.'

'Fuckin' simple Nicky. First off get a bird. Tell her write the giros, birds write better. Second, you want a bird pass the cheques, less aggravation. Then you got to have wheels get around out the area. Fuck knows Nicky, you always got the thinking, spoke Froggie good.'

'Don't need French sign a fuckin' giro Jimmy. Less you want to sign it in Calais.'

'You sort it Nicky. Now it's fuckin' two fifteen there ain't no time geezer, you got to get me down Upton Park so put them books up your strides eh?'

'Fair enough Jimmy,' I goes. 'Fair enough.'

'Get a butcher's them tubes Nicky, get a fix on which one comes out where so you can put 'em back in after.'

'Fair enough.'

'Let's go.'

So we went. Saturday afternoon, visitors all over the hospital, no one clocked Jimmy take a stroll. Took the tubes out – hurt him a bit – hid them under the pillow. Clothes were in the cabinet so we got his jeans and T-shirt on over the hospital morgue trousers. Put his trainers on him and fucked off out.

Got my dole money Friday so I had a few sobs, belled a cab out the front, booked him down the ground and back after. Jimmy fainted couple of times in the cab but nothing serious, got him a quick pint of lager and he was right as rain going in the ground. Had to hold him back final whistle, wanted to get down the pitch and up the Leeds bastards singing and spitting. Pulled him over, reminded him we got a cab. Went back up Whipps Cross and in bed time for tea. Never got the tubes back in the right places though, went the nurse I found him fell out of bed and all his tubes out. She gave me the look only I got scarce then. Noticed Jimmy just passed out again. Reckoned next time send someone else in case they made me one of the contracts, big hospital murderers came in to assassinate him. Went home.

Was sitting on the floor reading one of Marigold's books she came through the door. As usual bouncy.

'Hello Nicky.'

'Marigold, I used your dog and bone, hope you never mind.'

'Ring the Triads in Hong Kong?'

'Chingford and Leyton a few times.'

'I'll wear it. Have you had anything to eat yet?'

'Pay you back soon as I can Marigold, and all the nosh I ate, should get folding end of the week.'

'Don't be silly Nicky, it's not a problem. Anyway I might not want your money after where it came from.'

'Putting on a charity gig, honest, take a legit slice.'

Marigold made a noise half-way between a snort and a fart only she wouldn't make that.

'Yes? You sure Nicky? And no sidelines?'

Trouble with teachers was they got bright for a living.

'Marigold you reckon I can stay a bit longer? Like another week? Take till then sort everything. Go straight off now you want only next Sunday be handy. Total deadline.'

She thought on it.

'All right Nicky, since you're no trouble, I hardly know you're here and you're clean. Absolute deadline next

Sunday. You can't stay Sunday night even if there's squads of murderers outside the door. And nothing comes in here that isn't totally legit.'

'Marigold you're ace. You're a diamond. I loves you.'

'Yes well never mind all that. Where are we going tonight?'

'Pardon?'

'Well it's Saturday and the first time I've seen you all week and I haven't got anything booked so where are you taking me? Somewhere a bit exciting maybe? But I don't want any murders and I don't want any other major crimes either. What were you going to do tonight?'

'Video maybe, stay out the road. Daren't go up Walthamstow less I got multiple protection.'

'Would you go up Walthamstow with me?'

'Might do Marigold, on account of it'd be different places. What you fancy? Up the stadium? Teachers' boozer? Gambling house?'

'A gambling house please.'

Had to laugh. Not many schoolkids get the opportunity taking teacher up a gambling house. She took me up France, I took her up the gambling house on Grove Road.

First we ate Marigold's barley stew like a cornfield then went off out in Marigold's motor. Bleeding little Renault, hoped no one clocked me passenger in a little Renault. We went up Walthamstow on Grove Road, parked round the corner.

Big old house on the junction, blinds drawn, belonged an old biddy called Phoebe came over Barbados 1951. Floyd was on the door, doubled the British Legion would you credit.

'Hey-up Floyd.'

'Nicky who this young lady then?'

'She's my teacher.'

'She taught you real good eh, you teach him his living mam?'

'I did no such thing. I taught him to speak French.'

'You did? Not tell me he speak French. You speak French Nicky?'

'Not round here Floyd. How's business?'

'Business good. Go on down you want a play.'

Downstairs was puff and pool, one note a game, plenty noise but no stupidness not allowed. Middle floor was cards, seventy-nine and rummy and kaluki and brag. Upstairs was dominoes, plenty plenty noise there, got real heated but I never saw war. Five got you in the door then rum a nicker a tumbler or six a bottle probably went walkies off some container down Tilbury. Not heavy though, you wanted good-style shebeen you went up Clapton. Here was mostly old geezers over forty listening ska and reggae and rapping about cricket. Never clocked any of them in court.

Marigold and me we stood in line for a play on the pool, got loose with the rum, put dosh in the juke, Jimmy Cliff and Peter Tosh. No sweat. Two games pool then we went up watch the cards a while. Reckoned Micky Dressler not my problem, had to be a long way off.

Then I couldn't believe my porkies, who walked in?

DS fucking Grant that's who, out Chingford. Got his casuals on, stood out like a pig in a shebeen – not surprising come to think of it.

'Jesus fucking Christ!' I goes.

'That's me.'

'What the fuck you doing here?'

'Few words Nicky, want a few confidentials.'

'Fucking roll on. Confidential down some alley more like.'

Never give him the satisfaction asking how he clocked me there. Some grass owed him one saw me come in.

'Not like that Nicky, not like that at all, you know me.'

'Fuckin' right I do.' Turned to Marigold went "Scuse me, this here's DS Grant up Chingford, bent copper, specialises in Assault on Police. Lives up Epping, say no more.'

'Epping's a nice town Nicky. You his new bit of fluff miss?'

'And your gaff's out of nice Mr Freeman's, bit of graft here, bit of graft there. Fuckin' what you want DS Grant?'

'That's slander Nicky boy, you ought to know that. Anyhow I didn't come here to exchange pleasantries though I never knew you were a lover of cricket and darkie music. I want to exchange information with you.'

'And my grannie's a junkie.'

'Listen up Nicky, you could do yourself a favour know what I mean?'

'Yeah.'

'Them's big geezers Nicky, not playing canasta.'

'That like an aerosol?'

'That's canister. Canasta. Before your time. Listen up.'

'Fuck off.'

'You know anyone drives a Merc?'

'Me mum, me sister, all me mates.'

'Anyone doesn't have to lift it first?'

'Few dealers, few bent coppers.'

'There was a Merc round the estate the night Vinnie got it.'

'Plenty old Mercs round the estate.'

'A new one.'

'So?'

'We got the number. Someone belled us, no name. Can't finger anyone but thought you might like the number Nicky.'

'So?'

'It was seen down Canning Town, Silvertown area. We got it up Loughton too. K267 MML.'

Pause.

'Just thought you might be interested.'

'Thought I might get chopped more likely only bring them out same time. Fuck off DS Grant.'

'Only thought no point waiting for them coming to you Nicky. Be prepared I reckon. Just thought you might be interested that's all.' He gave a little wave like he thought he was the queen or maybe the commissioner. 'See you around Nicky.' Then he went for the door, every single punter knowing he was the Filth, keeping away like a bad smell.

Got hair sticking out his ears that DS Grant.

Soon after we went back home. I knew who got the motor, assuming DS Grant told it straight.

Roy Flowerdew. My brief.

'Jesus fucking Christ,' I went all the way home.

Marigold never said a lot.

'Rameez,' I went on the mobile, 'you never guess who brought them in, them fuckers.'

'Who Nicky?'

'Fucking Roy Flowerdew, my fucking brief. Brought in Micky Dressler them others. Set them up.'

'Jesus Nicky.'

'What we do Rameez?'

'Nothing Nicky, I reckon. We do nothing. We leave him for you. You got any conferences with him?'

'I ain't got nothing planned.'

'We deal the Asian Centre first then you got to account for him.'

'Your reckoning I got to account for everyone Rameez.'

'No harm. We doing business here Nicky.'

'Jesus Rameez. OK. Just wanted to know I do something.'

'Do nothing now Nicky. See how the cookie crumbles eh?'

'Right.'

We rang off.

Another one I got to account for. Wasn't easy life these days, you got to account for everyone.

Went to bed and tossed and turned. Then remembered what it was I never clocked down Roy's that conference. Roy he wanted to hear who I planned on manslaughtering, none of his business. Then he turned round and went how I used to put it up that Tina. Only he never was my brief days I put it up Tina. I got Mrs Mellow all cases round that time. So how come he knew? Hardly likely lawyers yakked on it lunchtime. More likely he knew I just went round. I was clocked, word got back.

So Roy was the jerk in the Merc got the dealers in. No wonder he got a big desk.

Wandsworth

Night my real dad left was a right one.

There was Dad or Slob see, like a stepdad, then before him there was my real dad.

Was about eight the time and Sharon was just a kid. Saturday night nine o'clock we were watching the box with Mum, probably some Yank Old Bill show. Then Dad came in steaming off the boozer, no one took notice, business as usual. Never caught on first off why he was home so early only he ran out of readies.

'Hey you,' he went Mum, 'where's me tea?'

'The oven.'

'Cold I reckon?'

'Clock goes six o'clock it's hot. Clock goes nine o'clock it's cold.'

'It's cold you cow, you fuckin' know it.'

Went out came back with his plate, turned round said 'Shift up,' me and Sharon. We shifted. Gobbed his grub went 'That was shit that was'. No one went a dickie. So he went 'Hey what these bleedin' kids doing up woman, don't you bleedin' look after them? Get up bed you little bastards, you won't get up school.'

'Don't go Sunday School,' I got to squeak. Big mouth even then.

Whacked me one. Mum went 'Leave that kid alone you

bleedin' great bully,' and he went 'Time these kids got a bit of respect and went to bed cow,' and went to whack her and I turned round and went 'Leave her alone you fuckin' moron,' although never knew what moron was and only vague idea about fucking. Sharon jumped in started bawling and Dad slung the plate at Mum, hit the ornaments on the side and all got a bit irregular. Not that special though till he went sudden 'I'm leaving. House'd drive a saint off, you listen?'

She went 'Mean you're going up that Michelle Joiner,' and he went 'What if I am cow?' She went 'Nothing only cheap slag her,' then he turned round and went 'What if she is bitch, least she reckons how to treat a geezer.'

Sharon and me we got pissed off went to watch the other box so they carried on. Last thing crash and he went out the door.

Mum couldn't believe he never came back. Not too fussed Sunday, glad to be shot of him only Monday blubbed before we went to school, blubbed dinnertime we came back then still leaking after school. Then we showed off on account of there was no tea. Then her friend Laila came over they both sat bawling then Mum reckoned she was going round after him only Laila went no way then Mum went anyway, reckoned she'd sort that Michelle Joiner. No joy natural. Dad he came back couple of times fetch his gear, like overalls and Elvis records, only they never spoke.

Me and Sharon we saw him now and then. They got the court in so some bird off the welfare came round asked questions then he took us up the fair or McDonald's Sundays. Used to wait on the corner and we went out all best clothes, Mum wanting to show we managed even he never sent the wedge like he was supposed to. So he got back buying burgers and milk shakes so we puked all up we got home. Worth it though.

Sometimes took us round his tart's, what Mum called her. That Michelle, she leered at us, gave us ice in our cokes only we always knew she wanted us like the lurgy. Never went there so often then it got so Dad never came every week even we were dressed and waiting, then Mum never got us dressed till he came then it dropped off altogether.

These days I clock him once in a while some boozer, gets me a lager, comes on all two-faced man-to-man. Bit fucking late that's his problem. Left his tart after a bit or got kicked out, depending who you listen up. They reckon he's with some bit up Stratford now. Lucky her, hope she's got a microwave.

So after a bit natural Mum took some fancy man.

Not straight away like months after, spent several weeks wailing she was some old piece furniture got thrown out. Then that Laila took her down bingo and the boozer, reckoned she got to get out of herself. First time she was so nervous sicked up her fish fingers before she left. Kept going did she look right, would they reckon she was a slag. First few times biggest thrill was her and Laila getting pissed four port and lemons down the club. Then one Friday would you believe, the Slob came round after her.

Looked like he sicked up his fish fingers too only with him it was every night.

Knew there was something going down on account of

she was hour and a half in the bathroom. Doorbell rang, Sharon got there like it was a fire alarm, Mum still in her chair. This geezer standing there thin as Aids about half as cheerful. 'Hey Mum,' went Sharon, 'there's some wimp here what does he want?'

They went off.

He gave her bits like, never whacked her. God knows they yakked about, I only heard if they wanted a cup of tea or got to wear a coat. First off she was never used to him didn't sling her about, reckoned there was something up. Then she got used.

Then he started slinking in watch a video cold nights. Sharon and me came in there they were the settee goggling *Fatal Attraction*. Blushed like they were torturing a few nuns.

Then he started parking on Dad's chair.

'Hey fat slob,' I went, 'that's me dad's place. Piss off out.'

'Now Nicky,' Mum went, he moved his arse, 'be nice to Henry he's a nice geezer.' Nice for fuck's sake! Henry for fuck's sake!

Then she got us together me and Sharon, reckoned she wanted to tell about him buying her bits and not belting her and that. 'What's he like in bed?' I went, like I heard up school only Mum never reckoned this high on the clapometer, whacked me round the fifth gear and the conversation never got any further.

Been married course and got used to his nights farting in front the video. She gave him the front door they reckoned on account of his cup of tea was more exciting he was. Sundays he took his kids down the canal, never knew how they lasted the pace.

We never got on.

So after about a year course Mum she got us in the front, sat us down went 'Now Nicky now Sharon I got to talk to you serious.' Long pause Sharon yawned like there might be something on TV soon. 'Look you kids, how you feel about getting a new dad?'

'Who we getting?' we went. 'Like we get to choose one?' Got a clue after Shithead started sleeping over only I reckoned maybe I could get someone off a video.

'Well Henry and me we was thinking of getting churched.'

'Suit yourself,' Sharon went. Bit broke up she was only made out she wasn't arsed. We were only yakking about what they did in bed, Sharon reckoned it made her sick thinking on the slob.

'But you got to be happy too,' Mum went, 'like he'll be part of the family.'

'Got a family.'

'And his feet pen and ink. And he drinks Martini. And he dog-ends his plate and he snores in the videos.' We were depressed. Mum she never snored and no more did Dad that matter. Nor drank Martini. So we hated the slob. Saturday night he got pissed on his Martini then she got pissed then we heard them snickering away the bedroom.

But they went down the registry course and life went on except now Shithead was there.

Then when Sharon got thirteen he started feeling her up.

Never told Mum and as it goes never told me a while

and he kept at her when Mum was on shift. Sharon reckoned he wanted to put it in her only she never let him.

Sharon gave me the news and I waited out his factory gate one Friday end of shift, went could I have a private word and that like. He was chuffed, reckoned I wanted a geezer-to-geezer so we went up the alley. Whipped out the CS canister gave him a bit up his nostrils so he lay down. Then he was still rolling about pulled his strides down poured some stuff over his hairy mick.

Don't know you'd reckon it, mixture everything out of chemistry. Only time I went in science that year, made up funny coloured mix everything I could find like they called a solution. Solution that little problem anyway, off hospital a fortnight they found him.

Gave it Mum he got mugged. Funny muggers went straight his Henry Halls, must have known he was a Henry maybe. She like believed him. Blistered so bad she reckoned it like the rainbow except it never went in an arch no more. Shithead he cottoned what it was down to, never gave Sharon more grief. That matter probably never gave Mum no more grief neither.

So Sharon got the club her sixteenth birthday she did it all alone. Least not all alone only he wasn't it.

Claimed she waited till it was legal. Me and several hundred knew different only no harm trying.

Ructions course. Mum wanting Sharon go to college do computers, Sharon going computers was finished; Shithead reckoned that a load of shit there was always jobs computers, so Sharon going he wanted to get his hooter out, he wasn't her dad. Mum went it wasn't sniffers she wanted keep out it was some other part, hadn't she heard?

It was Sunday breakfast, cartoons on TV.

She got the test Saturday down the market only never told Mum, wanted to go out Saturday night. It was her second test, never credited the first on account of she started the Pill. Only trouble was soon as she swallowed her first pill she reckoned she never got no worries. Mistake.

So there she was, hung over and we were on Sunday breakfast. Cigs and coffee and cartoons.

'I'm gonna get a kid,' she went, leaning on the cooker.

Mum dropped her coffee, broke the mug, scalded her foot, stained her slippers.

'Kid what?' she went. Not very bright remark come to think of it but first words came to mind.

'Kid black,' Sharon went,' what you reckon kid goat? Think yourself lucky it ain't Welsh.' Shithead was Welsh.

Mum sat down again white. Shithead stood up.

Mum went 'What?'

'You heard.'

'You had the test?'

'Yeah.'

'Jesus Christ.'

'He ain't got nothing to do with it.'

'Who you been seeing? I'll wring his neck.'

'Wring his dick more like,' Shithead went.

'You watch your own dick.' Couldn't turn round and say a lot to that, Mum still didn't hear about the other.

'How far you gone?' she went.

'Three months . . .'

'God Almighty.'

'You going to have it?' went Slob, still wouldn't shut it.

'Course I'm going to have it you filthy old fucker, not having no one muck about with me.'

'Muck about with you plenty when you have a kid,' Mum went. Then started leaking. 'Wanted you go to college do them computers be an air hostess.'

'Still do all that.'

'Like hell you will, I ain't looking after your kid while you fly round the world.'

'Anyway who wants frigging computers? I want someone love me computers never.'

'We all love you,' Shithead went.

'Yeah we know about you and loving. And no bleeder here loves nobody. This house like a fuckin' funeral parlour since me dad left.'

'That was years ago,' Mum went.

'You lot wouldn't know a good time if it ran up bit you in the bollocks.'

So it went on, they debated babies and computers. Me I went off for a quiet smoke. After a bit door slammed that was Shithead gone, then sniffles and tears that was Mum and Sharon blubbering together like women. Things still a bit sharp that night then couple of days everything normal again except Sharon started getting bigger.

Sharon got the kid September just after she heard she passed school exams. Her birthday was Boxing Day only I reckon her Kevin baby-father he gave it her for Christmas.

Then me I shacked up Kelly a bit. Got the kid with her, I reckoned give it a trial. Never let on she was getting a kid only there it was, popped out. Went it was something to do with me. Well I went, maybe I put it in there only like I always say babies are down to them.

All the same no objection having a kid, good little bleeder. She's too soft on him, he only takes notice of me. I'm away he gets off with it. Soon be playing football, robbing car cassettes. Only joking, bound to be a brain surgeon.

So she got the kid, got a flat off the housing, I moved in a bit. Stripped the walls all that game, got given bits of furniture, cooker and strip of carpet, then got to nick curtains and bedclothes on account of the Social don't pay out these days. Not so simple nicking right size curtains, got to get measurements then never just swanny off with an armful. Went up the warehouse Saturday afternoon, made the choice then back Saturday night had them away. Jimmy Foley rode the van for me.

Was with her on and off six months. No remission good behaviour. Advantages you get it when you feel like only disadvantages like she wants it she feels like and a geezer doesn't always feel like. Then there's your freedom, like I go off few days she makes it her business know where I'm off. Like I say did all the stripping and painting, doesn't follow I'm doing life, know what I mean?

Then she got an Uncle Bob. VDU operator, learned it school or somewhere. Good wedge. Seemed to reckon made me look after little Danny. Pulled that one out her box, plotted it her mum most likely. Gone eight in the morning not back till six, by then little Danny's shitted himself four times, got his bottle three times, gone asleep twice, driven me up the wall ten times. Don't get me wrong I'm domestic only a feller wants to choose when or get down the boozer, Danny not into boozers yet.

Mind like I say I'm better the kid than what she is – more firmer. Does how I tell him. Not getting hooked on her caper though so I turned round and went how I got working too. Who you? she went and pigs might fly so I nearly smacked her only little Danny was there. So I got out couple of sessions behind the bar the club down Billet stop her winding me up. Got the kid a minder in the block, some bird already got three others. Good earner minding kids, only trouble is four kids means sixteen shits a day.

Little Danny loves his dad I always bring him a present, least when I can. Not going to disappear like my fucking real dad.

Chapter Nine

I called a meeting up the Sportsman on Markhouse. Booked their upstairs got a bar. Many the time I put one up some bird the toilets there in some disco. This time strictly business. Put the word round everyone several days, got them there Monday night eight o'clock.

There was Wayne Sapsford came after daily reporting up Chingford, before his curfew. There was Darren Boardman the accumulator and Sean Loveless my mate from McEntee. There was Sharon's baby-father Kevin Elliott and there was Elvis Littlejohn all the birds got wet over. There was little Lotus Lennie Tack and Mercedes Marty Fisherman and Dean Longmore, each nicked a motor parked on Queen's. There was Brendan Streeter done well lived up Tudor Court over the road. There was Salim Butt worked in computers still liked his Saturday nights. Then there was the birds, reckoned we got to have them, no choice. Sharon I never called, never wanted her involved. Never ask Kelly obvious reasons. There was Julie Seagrave always ready on a good scrap, there was

Shelley Rosario trailing after that Elvis, there was Paulette
James grew up to be an athlete, not so bad after all she got
up that sand dune before me. Got her a message through
that Tina and she rolled up last minute. Then that Tina
came, couldn't stop her. Made fifteen with me.

Most of us went school together or youth centre down
Leyton. Not all mates, half of them I had serious mischief
with and other half all screwed each other only this was
Walthamstow and we got to stick together now. Knew
they were there no danger. Even the tarts were there,
got to be.

Never clocked a meet like it. Never had a meeting
before, none of us knew how to get started. So we lifted
few bottles rum seemed like a good start, various places
down Lea Bridge. Bought the Coke over the bar, never
wanted to look cheap. Got a few cracks each then I made
the move get started.

'Fuckin' shut it you lot,' I went loud.

They shut it mostly, some of them.

'Fuckin' we got to get a plan,' I went.

'Fuckin' what up Nicky?' goes Julie Seagrave. 'You give
me the call, reckoned it Vinnie's business we got to sort it.
What happening Nicky?'

'Yeah what happening?' goes Dean Longmore, probably got the fidgets – half-hour since he nicked a motor.

Brendan and Elvis and Kevin stayed cool. Others went
'Yeah what happening man?'

Got up made a speech.

'Fuckin' shut it,' I went again. Never reckoned how
else to start. Then I went how it all happened on Vinnie
and Jimmy Foley still up Whipps Cross even took a turn
after the football went in intensive few hours. Mentioned
Rameez they all shit themselves only glad he was on our

side. Then I went how we got to grease him and pay Jimmy's and pay the Centre and then we got to get ready an affray grand-style when Micky and Errol and Andrew showed. Told how Rameez was booking the Asian Centre big-style.

They all shut it till I finished.

Then they all went 'Fuck me Nicky fuck me man.'

'Fucking fuck me Nicky,' went Sean Loveless. 'I'm in man. Fuckin' shitless but I'm in man.'

'We're in,' went Julie and Shelley. Fucking lot of use most situations birds only Shelley was a working girl up King's Cross these days could earn a few, Julie like I say was a scrapper.

'Get the dosh right quick,' went Dean. 'No problem.'

'Drive round on the giros,' went Marty. 'Be a pleasure.'

'One thing Nicky,' went Brendan.

'Yeah we know,' went Sean.

'You know what?'

'You no thief.'

'Correct man. I no thief. Salim also.'

'I working,' goes Salim. 'Anyway I no thief sorry. I with you up the Asian Centre no problem.'

'Me also,' goes Brendan. 'I with you up there for Vinnie Nicky, no problem.'

'Yeah I know that,' I goes.

So we cracked another bottle and we planned.

Birds wrote out the giros. Used to be you only got £50 no ID only now it was £150 you're lucky. No point chancing it though so they made out mostly £80 or £90. Reckoned it all got to be same day before they got the message, two geezers one bird each motor. One Kent one Hertfordshire. Any aggravation any post office they left quick. Take envelopes and stamps and post the dosh straight off only not outside the post office they just done. Told them all post it their mum's. Any left over after was commission.

That was Dean and Kevin and Julie then Marty and Lennie and Tina. Paulette she never said only we knew she never thieved like Brendan and Salim, too busy running for England or somewhere. Shelley went she could go down the Cross raise a half no problem.

Sean and me we planned the clothes shops. Kids' stuff only it was quick dosh maybe a thou.

Wayne booked up north Chingford round the station. Car phones, reckoned he could lift twenty half an hour, quick stuff then away. Few hundred.

Darren and Elvis reckoned they knew some geezer up Comet leave the back door open, twenty videos was a thou easy.

We were planned.

'Then fuckin' how you going to get them there Nicky, them geezers?' went Sean.

'Yeah then fuckin' how you going to get them there Nicky?' went the rest.

'You all going to put the word round,' I turned round and went. 'You all going to tell the world we taking over and we doing a very big deal Friday up the Asian Centre. Very big business, smack and crack and whatever. You aren't saying no difference to nobody. All they hear is we're taking over and we start there. Big dope, big deals, big geezers.'

'They frightened on that?' went Elvis.

'They frightened. I going to shoot one.'

Was a long sigh like gasp came from all round. I going to shoot one.

Andrew Okema stood there mean.

'What you want kid?' he asked. 'Why you bothering me this time of day? Haven't I seen you before? Haven't I warned you off here before?'

Wasn't a dawn raid on account of I never could get up for dawn. It was nine o'clock, after breakfast.

Three days since I went round Brian Dear, belled him on his mobile fixed an appointment. Got there told him I wanted a shooter. Offered a wedding party in the bargain only I went I never wanted the whole package just a shooter please.

Asked what sort I wanted so I went something more likely hit the other geezer than me, like two metres away. Offered me an airgun only joking then a sawnoff do a bit of damage. Told him a bit awkward hiding it on the bus. He went then it got to be a Browning nine millimetre.

'You want black or brown?' he went.

'Shit Brian you ask me. Them the only choices?'

'Less you want to paint it. Get you brown, I got more in stock. Meet you down the car park two o'clock do a bit of practice. Bring a three.'

Those days the car park over Chingford Hall had a roof on it. No one took notice a few gunshots. Brian was waiting round the corner, came in soon as I arrived.

'All right Brian.'

'All right Nicky, you got the fee?'

'Fee's here Brian.' Gave him the three hundred.

'Lookin' good Nicky. Now this here's a shooter.'

Looked like a shooter to me too. Looked like a big shooter could shoot a hole in a house.

'Brian,' I went, 'I never get that in my pocket man.'

'Down your waistband Nicky fuck's sake not your pocket. And not down the front or you likely shoot your dick off. Down the back nice and easy no problem.'

'Jesus. How many shots I got Brian?'

'Fourteen shots Nicky. One up the spout you want is fifteen. You want to shoot a geezer though always best you shoot him with the first one. Might get upset you stand there take fifteen shots at him, think you're taking liberties. Maybe we get some practice in eh?'

'Thanks Brian.'

'So where you want to shoot him?'

Bit of a question that. Anywhere suited me. Best plan was a kneecapping or down the calf IRA-style, nice clean job but they know you mean the business. Problem was IRA they held them down for the occasion, and not likely Andrew Okema wanted being held down. Didn't suit to kill him for the plan. Bit of a problem.

'Aim for the foot Brian,' I went.

'Just a scratch eh, let him know you're around.'

'Like that.'

'You know how you point the thing?'

'Heard you point it the other geezer.'

'Always best.' He put it in my mitt, good job I kept up the weight training. We went off up a quiet corner.

'Start the beginning Nicky,' he went. 'You know what the safety is?'

'Prefer you take it off now Brian and it stays off. Wouldn't like forget it try shooting him only get nowhere. Difficult situation.'

'How long you reckon you're going to walk round carrying it with the safety off?'

'Day maybe two. That OK?'

'You're gonna shoot yourself. Best option is you put it somewhere very safe then pick it up just before you do the bit of work. Be all right then long as you're careful. Understood?'

'Understood Brian. Somewhere very safe then I be all right long as I'm careful.'

'Now I show you how to shoot the fucker eh?'

So we went and practised then he loaded it up full and one up the spout then he took the safety off and I went up Mum's put it under my bed. Told Sharon not let the kid in there. Picked it up the big day carried it gentle up Chingford Hall.

♦

'What the hell you want?' went Andrew Okema. 'I'm losing my patience man.'

'Come to tell you and Micky and Errol,' I went. 'We taking over the business.' No point getting into further discussion so then I shot him in the foot.

Matter of fact, I aimed his right foot hit his left. Probably on account of how I was shaking like in a hurricane. No one knew which one I aimed though so no problem.

'And that for Vinnie too,' I went. Nearly forgot. He was doubled roaring by then so I pissed off.

Pretty soon they'd be finding who was Vinnie's mate again. Could be they'd shoot up Mum's only I hoped they took more notice what I said on the business angle. Find out where we meant doing business and listen up the tales spreading round the manor now we put the word out serious.

◆

Belled Rameez on the mobile to his mobile, told him the score.

'You done good Nicky,' he went. 'How you feeling man? You feel hot?'

'Feel shit tell the truth Rameez. Getting out the borough now. You got the Centre Friday?'

'No problem. Absolute no problem. Centre booked, found a charity also. Leukaemia on account of them kids you know one Asian one white recent? Good cause Nicky, make me proud give them their slice. Everything lined up, every religion in the borough coming.'

'Right.'

'You sure you OK Nicky? You not sounding too sharp man.'

'Never said I felt sharp Rameez, said I felt shit. No more shooters OK?'

'OK Fine. Only you're a big man now Nicky Burkett, everyone gets to know. You lined my cash?'

'No problem. You probably heard everyone out getting it.'

'I heard. You're a good man Nicky, man of your word.'

'Too shit-scared of you do otherwise Rameez.'

'Hah! Joking of course. We getting lined up too, me and my men.'

'Be in touch Rameez.'

'See you later Nicky.'

I went back Marigold's, spent the day sleeping and listening up French music. Never slept the night before too fucking nervous so got a bit of making up now. It felt better.

◆

Then later that night I was asleep on the floor in front the video. Marigold doing school work, supping wine. We ate earlier she came in, more cornfields. She was ace that Marigold.

'Nicky,' she goes close up my ear. 'Bedtime. It's midnight.'

'Uh.' She was kneeling beside me, right close. I put a hand round her neck before I could stop. Drew her mouth on top of mine. Even then reckoned Christ, you blew it now, Nicky, only Christ she kissed me! Soft on the lips, round my top lip round the bottom then moved her tongue in. Christ. Ran it round my teeth, on my gums on my tongue. Christ.

'Christ,' I went.

She lay down next to me on the floor then moved on top, lying on me. I was awake now. She moved up to gob me more, I put my mitts on her back under her top, up and down like. No bra. She opened her legs, got trousers on, moved against me moved up me, kissed me again like before then kissed round my face eyes nose ears neck. Undid my shirt kissed my chest, did it again stomach and shoulders, bit my tits. Christ. So I took her top off over her head and her tits came to my gob, first one then other. Her breath drew short. Got lovely tits, fit and round.

I started saying something only she put the finger on my teeth, drew me up, took me down my bedroom. She wanted it there, keep hers sacred. Stood in front of me half-naked, smiled, I smiled, grinned. Then she took the rest off. Me too.

She pulled the bed things off. We got on the bed on our sides, touched. We put one arm over each other and I laughed and we kissed and I was on top of her, half over then in between. She looked up smiled, we rolled over she was on top. She was warm her body and her skin it made me want to come on its own. We rolled back kissing and my leg got between hers and I felt her wet against my thigh.

'Christ,' I went.

She sort of chuckled.

Then she was back on top and it got serious, she ran her tongue down my belly and her tits across me. Christ.

'Mmm I like your penis,' she went. She was in position to form an opinion on it. Then she moved quick, rubbing up me again kissing on the lips.

Clocked myself going 'Oh!' like surprised. I wasn't used all this, it was A-level fucking. Like this was what they did up Stoke Newington it was brilliant.

'Oh!' I goes again.

Then she moves further up and believe she kneeling over my gob. 'Uh' I goes. Then I hold her hips and she lowers herself and she gasps when she touches me. I move my tongue up, find her there, move it round then she's away again. I follow her, we're on our sides again then I kiss her tits and her thighs then run my tongue up inside her thigh till I find her again wet and soft. She gasps again and holds my bonce there then she moves it away again and brings me up to kiss her on the mouth. 'Nicky,' she goes very softly.

Then she rolls on me again, moves down tits all over me then she licks it, licks it all round till I cry then takes it easy into her mouth all the way in like she loves it. Just a moment then she's off again.

Moves up me and we've got arms round rolling over and back.

Then I know I got to do it. So I goes down on her, she opens her thighs pulls her knees back and when I touch her she's nearly there already. I lick up through her till I find her and it's there. I lick it backwards and forwards, first slowly then quicker then quicker still then sudden there's a little pulse goes once, twice, I can feel it. Then away she arches up, holds my head then she sits up upright cries out Oh, Oh, softer Oh, then she arches again then she lies back shaking, going with it rocking side to side, loving it friends with it letting it roll, gradually dying down then laughing, laughing. I lie up beside her and she hugs me.

'Oh Nicky,' she goes eventual, 'that was something wasn't it? Will you come inside me later with a condom please, then I can come again? That was lovely Nicky.'

'Sounds the biz Marigold,' I go and we're both laughing. 'Sounds the biz.' She hugs me again. 'Who'd have thought,' she goes, 'when you were a little kid with all your snotty little mates, who'd have thought it?'

'Not me Marigold.' And I hugs her. Knew it made no difference she still wanted me out the flat only it never mattered. Knew I couldn't handle all that every night anyway. Bleeding great a night or a week even only then a geezer gets knackered just thinking on it. Never got to do all that with Kelly any road, she probably reckoned all that was dirty. Just a straight bit was all she wanted. All she was going to get anyway.

Went to kip very big smiles on my bonce. So did Marigold, I felt it on my shoulder. Nodded off. I slept like a baby. She was brilliant that Marigold, even more brilliant I ever reckoned.

Wandsworth

We got a grass last week in here.

Nonces and grasses are on forty-three generally. Nonces fucked their kids or raped some old bag. Some rapes don't get a real hard time, maybe just put their bird in order or had some bit outside a club, no big deal. Most get whacked though. Grasses similar. Grass up someone gets sent the same nick, it's a big bruise job. Grass up someone there in nick say goodbye your bollocks.

Mind there's grassing and grassing. Like when Abdul stuck himself I never could right sit there watch him go off to Mecca. Had to squeal. But squeal the screws on some aggravation up the recess or bit of crack on visits, well out of order so you're like brown bread.

Got to take care mess orderlies. Some redbands are sweet, like governor's orderly tell you anything and old-time cons never grass their worst enemy. Only got to wonder though young cons no special reason being mess orderly and then they get extra visits or special de-cat. Don't give out chat their way.

This one we got though he was rat's arse on the out. Came Bristol so they moved him up here out the way, never reckoned Bristol's like five minutes up the motorway these days. Would you credit next cell to little

Wallace was geezer off same estate, up London got a piece of work some chassis merchant and got lifted. But his last sentence was burglaries and who was it grassed him up but little Wallace.

They had him on the wing not the seg so no one guessed, only not very clever they put him in next someone else down Bristol. Must have clocked it was funeral time soon as he laid his beadies on his mate there.

Thursday on association was when we took him, always plenty of noise off *Top of the Pops*. So we got him in the shithouse, kicked fuck out of him.

Lost three teeth and bent his sniffer. Then someone cracked his jaw got to be wired, six weeks. Matter of fact I was never too fussed getting involved what with release date coming up never wanted to lose time. Can't afford to turn it down though or lose your rep. So I booted him couple of times or three. They found him at bang-up and he's still up the hospital at taxpayers' expense so he got a result after all.

No hard feelings on little Wallace only he finished up the wrong nick and you got to whack him. Nonces though that was different. All sorts in here, beasts, molesters, baby killers. Got to find ways on getting them. Then again there's enough GBH merchants and malicious woundings must be plenty to choose out of for whacking nonces. Or there's other ways not only whacking. Lump of shit looks good in the dinner, piss in their tea gives it flavour. Screws never give a toss, even once in a while they leave a nonce alone and not on the forty-three. Have a bit of sport strawberry jam-style.

One other way's get down the block yourself on discipline. Sometimes no choice you find your way down there. Tell one screw fuck off and you're on reports, tell another fuck off or maybe refuse work and it's down the block. Assault on screw don't even think about it, down the block and lose time in the bargain. Serious error of judgement. Only consolation is down the block you get reasonable chance on whacking nonces.

Two sorts of block so take your pick, three counting suspended. CC and it's no papers, books, radio and privileges, fact is you're fucked. But get a bit of GOAD and it's like unofficial. Nick you only they never prove anything so they reckon few days good order and discipline sort you out. Get radio and papers and a bit of a breather, then sometimes you get association down there. Problem is you associate nonces and grasses, then again get the opportunity whack a few and help your rep.

Done it a few times, me. Best was some creepy geezer around fifty-five reckoned he was in for burglary only the screws told us he shafted little girls. Got him on the way back off visits when they were short-staffed, cracked his hooter, put a bit of blood round. Best part is they never fight back nonces.

Never really wanted get involved this grass though like I say. Due for release two weeks don't want to go losing time on account some poxy grass. Fortunate though, they got the Bill in seeing it was GBH only they never found anything so I was clean.

♦

Now last two weeks of my sentence they put me in with this thin black geezer. So thin he never ate. So mean he never dickied a word. Only reason I knew he wasn't total dumbo was when he first came in he clocked the walls, clocked me, then went 'You wanna know something? You full of shit man.' Then he lay down on the bed three days never opened his gob.

Had one piss three days and I know for a fact never shit. Nor ate that matter so maybe he never needed shitting. Never got off the bed except the one piss. Refused exercise. Refused slop-out. Refused canteen. I sat there watched his beard grow. Slowly. That was how I discovered black geezers' beards grow slower than white geezers'. Even slower you allow for it curling round.

Third day I brought *L'Équipe* back from papers. Eyes followed me round the cell. I lay down, read the paper. Silence about a minute i.e. business as usual. Then he turned round and said:

'You fuckin' read French geezer?'

Nearly fell off the bed only I just went 'Course I fuckin' read French what you think I just look at the pictures?'

'Fuckin' I get banged up with a nintellectual. You wanna go Africa with me?'

'Tonight? I'm booked man.'

'Don't shit me droophead. You wanna go Africa with me or you not wanna go Africa with me?'

'I not wanna go Africa with you.'

'Oh.'

'How long you doing?'

'Two.'

'Just got weighed off?'

'You said it.'

'You want to get conditional release you better start

eating friend. They don't give jam roll people don't eat
or shit or talk. They like regular geezers, no danger to
the community. Start shitting and talking you're out
automatic one year.'

'How long you?'

'Six. Two weeks left.'

'For?'

'Slaughter.'

'That's cool.'

He was so cool I wanted thermals. 'Anyway Marcus
Garvey,' I went, 'where is it I fit in your holiday plans?'

'You translate me.'

'Translate you? Missed Zulu our school. No call for it.'

Gave me the hard stare, looked at first like another
three days the big chill. Then he went 'Africa they speak
French'.

'Run that by me? They speak French? Where?'

'Senegal.' He closed his meat pies respect for Senegal.

'Who's she?'

Opened them again, swung his legs off the bed, violent
activity. 'Senegal!' he went. 'You shitting me man?'

'Negative.'

'In Africa,' he went like a speech, 'they speak French,
except some retarded areas they speak English. This my
heritage. You may translate me till we learn them real
African languages.'

'How long it all takes brother? I'm in demand you
appreciate. What's your name anyway?'

'Slip. Take two or three.'

'Slip? Two or three what?'

'Slip my name. Two or three years. I looking up my
ancestors.'

'Slip some French name?'

'Ain't French fatso, course not. My daddy from Jamaica innit? Only my mother she born Guadeloupe and she speak French till she three. Forgot it all now. Her grandmother or maybe before that she reckon came out of Senegal. She a slave prob'ly. I aim finding out. Do business there trace my ancestors same time.'

'Business? What the thieving like Senegal?'

'Shit you,' he went. 'Shit you man. You steal off a brother in Senegal and I cut your dick off.'

'How else you live there?'

'Compact discs man. You aware Senegal ain't got many CDs yet? And them personal computers? And clothes, modern gear like out the shops London?'

'Now you're talking,' I goes. 'My speciality clothes shops. Only you sure there much demand CDs and personals? They want them out Africa?'

'You got to create the demand brother! You never read Karl Marx? Capitalism depend on creating demand, ripping off the brothers! Only sorry I got to do it so I find my ancestors. Remember it production for profit not need and workers do not get the fruits of their labours. Well we got to get the fruits daddy!'

Sounded fair enough to me. Only one other thing though. 'Hey Slip,' I went.

'Yeah?'

'What you in for?'

Mumbled 'Import . . .'

'How you get lifted?'

Mumbled.

'Spill it man, how you get lifted?'

'Went Jamaica. Bought coconut export licence. Filled them coconuts with weed man. The man told customs. Got lifted Heathrow.'

'Grassed up!'

'Not funny brother. First trip too on my daddy's homeland. Jamaica was cool man.'

There I was planning biggest deals this side Hong Kong and turns out my partner got turned in on a coconut.

'Still,' I went, 'Jamaica coconut licence could be useful exporting CDs England to Africa. Make a start.'

'Don't shit me droophead.'

'They got big sand dunes Africa?'

'Like to tell.'

'Best thing I ever beadied was this sand dune in Froggie. Reckon Africa got to have sand dunes. What's the birds like?'

'Married.'

'Shit.'

'You coming man?'

'Coming. Got to help you find your grannie. And got to be some birds. And I got to get a tan.'

Plans.

Chapter Ten

I was sleeping quiet up Marigold's when the pager went.

Got to be Mum. No one else got the pager number and up ten o'clock the morning.

Message on the pager went went 'Ring Mum you little bleeder'.

Never wanted Mum belling the mobile running me down too easy. So I kept the pager never gave her the mobile number.

I got up off the mattress a bit bleary, found the dog and bone, rang Mum.

'This is the *Walthamstow Guardian*,' I went, polite like, 'wishes to ask your opinion on the coming Council elections and the prospects on the dogs tonight up the Stow.'

'Piss off you little bleeder,' she goes. 'You got your appointment up the Probation.'

'Shit.'

'Don't use that language on me Nicky just get your arse

up there. I found the letter off them.'

'Found it hunting out my drawers I reckon.'

'Never you mind where I found it only get yourself up there, you ain't nothing only bleeding wotless Nicky.'

'No call getting aerated over that Andy up Probation Mum. No call getting upset. Still be there tomorrow.'

Only no point getting up his nose too far though so I belled Rosie up their office.

'All right Rosie,' I goes, 'this is Nicky. You reckon what time I got an appointment that Andy?'

'Twenty minutes ago Nicky, he just came out here bad-mouthing you.'

'Tell him don't get out his pram Rosie, I'll be there straight up. Tell him I got diet problems held me up.'

'Don't steal no car to get up here Nicky. Use the bus service and be a few minutes later.'

'You get that about the diet Rosie?'

'Nicky do yourself a favour just get up here eh?'

There I was busy as a bastard trying to get everything sorted for the big trouble and I got to get up Probation. I hoped that Andy got the kettle sorted.

Got a cab on account of I never liked nicking motors out the borough. Rolled in there thirty minutes later still never got a cup of tea yet. Went in reception found a few bodies all looked like they wanted a cup too. Dean Longmore keeping busy, daily reporting up Chingford only came in Probation after a sandwich. Young kid Kamran and a lifer name of Lou. Black footballer Alvin and crackhead called Louise did a bit of kiting. No smoking in there so they all got withdrawal.

'All right Rosie?' I goes.

'All right Nicky,' she goes drinking her coffee one hand hitting the WP the other. 'Tell Andy you're here only he's got someone with him now. Saw your mum up the market the other day.'

'What she got to say?'

'She reckoned you were more trouble than your little Danny.'

I had to cackle. 'Eats more than me though got to say.'

'Prettier than you too I reckon.' Switchboard kept ringing so she got answering and hitting the WP and sipping her coffee and combing her hair out. 'You spare any of that coffee Rosie?' I turned round and said.

'Reckon you only come up here on a cup of coffee,' she went, pushing it through the window.

'And see you Rosie, you knows that.'

'And talk plenty of brango. What is it this time Nicky, Andy doing a report on something you never done of course?'

'How'd you know Rosie? Got stitched up. Yuck it ain't got no sugar in it.'

Then Andy came through the door seeing off some punter, old geezer I never clocked like maybe some bank robber. 'Morning Nicky,' he goes. 'Sorry to disturb you from your bed but nice of you to turn up I suppose.'

'Sarcasm is the lowest form of wit Andy,' I turns round and says. 'I was so exhausted and cream crackered by my efforts to keep within the law that I laid behind the clock for a few minutes. Excuse me Rosie,' I goes, handing over the coffee, 'I got to see the man.'

'Hope he talks some sense into you Nicky.'

We went through Andy's office where he stashed the kettle. He switched on and pushed over the biscuits, more of the health crap.

'Saw you up West Ham Saturday,' he goes, 'only I thought Jimmy Foley was in Whipps Cross?'

'Jesus you make yourself busy Andy,' I went, 'spend your weekends looking me up eh?'

'Spend my weekends down West Ham trying to forget about you, only it seems impossible. Fair match eh?'

'Not bad Andy, not bad. Shoot straighter myself only not bad.'

'Shoot straighter with some shooter off Brian Dear maybe.' Jesus, what was he earwigging? Pushed me the coffee went 'Now then Nicky, you know I've got to do another report on you.'

'Yeah I reckon. Only what case Andy?'

'Going equipped.'

'Oh yeah. Nothing only stupidness Andy, you know that. Going equipped shit, some copper wanted a nicking boost his arrests so he got on my case.'

'And you pleaded guilty.'

'Got to Andy, course I went guilty carrying some screwdriver yeah I'm equipped. Equipped on a bit of carpentry too only don't mean I'm lifting no motor middle of the day up Hoe Street half the town looking.'

'But were you intending to lift a motor?'

'Now don't get personal Andy, you're digging me out here. Reckon I was on my way up the snooker hall. Got pulled. Happen to anyone.'

He got his pad out. 'So I'll say you admit the offence and will face whatever sentence the court imposes but had nothing specific in mind. All right?'

'Fair enough Andy, fair enough.' I sipped on the coffee, took another biscuit. 'Fuck me Andy,' I went spluttering, 'where'd this coffee come from? Malaria?'

'Nicaragua Nicky. Now shut up a bit and think what

they're going to do with you. You're in a spot of bother as you know, might not be so serious but you've got a fair record eh?'

'Bit of form,' I went modestly.

'And if you come in front of that Mr Rodber again he might want to hang you by the short and curlies.'

'Only that's where your report comes in Andy innit, mitigating circumstances, hard life and you make some constructive proposals like.'

He gave me the looks-could-kill look.

'Only your words Andy, got me a touch on that last one, hundred hours community work and that. No chance a spot of probation here this time I suppose, make a change?'

'Not bloody likely. Prefer to do my worrying over West Ham and the rainforests thank you Nicky, without having you as well. How did that Community Service go last time then?'

'Fucking brilliant Andy. Fucking brilliant.'

'Eh? Doing what then?'

'Well first off they put me on some wind-up, some work party only I blew that one straight out, no danger. Got a sick note, allergic to paint, he even went allergic to groups in the bargain the doc. So they put me up by old Mrs Shillingford on Greenleaf Road, fucking brilliant woman.'

'Doing what?'

'Well, did her bit of garden like. Fucking gave me blisters, you ever tried that gardening? So then she got me busy round her house was all. Got me cooking. Fucking brilliant woman. Eighty-seven, blind as a bat, stuck in her chair, got me making the old yam and sweet potato stews for her. She sat there told me the doings.

You want the recipe Andy? Molasses, tomato, onion and plenty plenty hot sauce. And yam and sweet potato you reckon.'

'Thanks for the tip Nicky. And you managed to complete the order?'

'No worries. Let me alone. Never even knew it finished till they turned up six months later. Couldn't wait Saturdays. Went round Sundays in the bargain, clean up her gaff. Then she sits there yakking on her old boyfriends in Dominica and the carnival back she was seventeen. Fucking ace. Get me back on the community work round hers Andy no problem. Still go round Sundays for me dinner anyway I want.'

'Only one problem there Nicky, Community Service isn't supposed to be your leisure activity or they'd have you stealing cars for yours. So how often do you still go round Mrs Shillingford's?'

'Any week I never commit no crimes Andy.'

'Pardon?'

'She reckons I can come round Sunday dinner I never commit no crimes that week.'

'Jesus. How does she know?'

'I tells her.'

'You tell her the truth?'

'Do me a favour Andy. Fucking brilliant woman Andy, I never tell her no porkies.'

'Wonder you haven't killed her with shock then. So how often do you get a clean week?'

'Maybe once a month. I bells her Saturdays things are looking good.'

'Must be the bloody answer. Clean up London. Perhaps she'd like to be a probation officer Mrs Shillingford.'

'Fit you in too Andy, you want. Go round Mrs

Shillingford Sundays, fit you in Saturdays. Clock them kids of yours.'

'Like I say Nicky, I try to spend my Saturdays forgetting all about you. Anyway you're always two hours late for appointments, miss your meal by that time.'

'Keep appointments weekends Andy no problem. Only weekdays is difficult.'

'And I heard you were getting pretty busy on weekends these days Nicky, what's this about you and the Asian Centre this Friday?'

'Eh?'

'Heard you were organising some gig up the Asian Centre?'

'Your earholes working overtime Andy?'

'Word gets about. So what's the story?'

'Goodwill Andy, goodwill is all, give an assist up the cripples.'

'Pull the other one Nicky it's got bells on. How much on the scam?'

'Only a tenper Andy, the usual tenper or maybe twenty, cover expenses, you got to. Sell you a ticket?'

'Not bleeding likely. I might give the money to the family maybe but not through your mitts.'

'Dear oh dear Andy, no charity. You're marking my card before I ain't done nothing.'

'Not long before. Bet you don't have dinner round Mrs Shillingford's this Sunday.'

I laughed. Got to cackle. No answer really.

So we went for the community work on that going equipped I nearly forgot about and he promised have a word see I could get back up by Mrs Shillingford. I finished my coffee account of he had to get up some meeting.

Matter of fact going equipped never did get dealt with.

Overtaken by events. Reckon eventually they just ditched it, too boring to take back to court.

♦

Went out Probation up the road, got on Hoe Street, reckoned it was time for a pattie. Got about as far as the radio shop.

Whack. Got coated off like I never been coated. Back of the knee and I was flying.

Whack again. I was rolling so they never hit where they meant. Got me up the arse like a bus hit it. Christ.

I was scrabbling hard only I knew one hit like that on the bonce and I was out of it. I was panicked. I was shitting. This was it.

Then sudden there were other noises, there was geezers whacking each other. I tried getting up, couldn't on account of the knee. Dragged in a doorway near screaming, looked back on the street. Rameez to the rescue, him and Aftab and Javed and a couple. Got more numbers than the geezers coating me off with the baseball bats. Rameez and his posse got rice flails and crowbars, they were mean. One geezer sleeping on the floor blood coming out his nose. Three others disappearing fast.

'You stand Nicky?' went Rameez.

'No. Fuck me Rameez I was dead there I was a dead man. You watching out for me?'

'Watching out for you Nicky.' He was hyper and panting, they all were. 'Get you out of here.' Cavalier pulled up one of his posse driving. Took us all away quick down Greenleaf, up Forest and back Rameez's family home. No one in except his sister, very delicious bird only I wasn't thinking that now. They carried me in till the dead leg got over it. Like if it got over it it wasn't bust.

'Fuck me Rameez geezer, I was a dead man. Reckon I owes you the lot.' Lay on the sofa heart still pounding and they gave me tea and codeine.

'We was watching out for you Nicky. What you been up Probation?'

'Yeah.'

'Reckon they watching out for you too. Best you don't go round the signing on or the boozers or the street this week Nicky. They watching out man, looking to get you.'

'You too now geezer.'

'I protected. Safe a few days. Then we gets them.'

'We wish. Jesus Rameez I owes you.'

'Mention it. I protecting my investment. Five Friday, you remember?'

'Not forget I owes you five K Rameez. Jesus that hurts now.'

'Feeling coming back in Nicky. Reckon you going to be OK. No feeling you got a problem. Feeling coming back just hurts, fuckin' painful is all.'

'Jesus Rameez.'

Wandsworth

Mum came on a visit up Feltham five days after I got remanded. They kept me Feltham till I got twenty-one, then transfer up Brixton.

'You bleedin' done it now Nicky,' she goes.

'Leave it out Mum,' I goes.

'Christ Nicky you killed him you bleedin' killed him.'

'Fuck's sake Mum.'

'And none of that language. Wasn't much of a geezer Nicky, never did you no favours only you never got to turn round and kill him.'

I had to laugh. Never slept two nights police cells, never slept five nights up Feltham, sick every day, never ate, not only I wasted the geezer and facing life in the bargain, now Mum reckons I stuck him on account of he never did me no favours.

'Jesus Mum,' I turned round and said.

'Want a fag?' she went.

'Yeah.'

Then she started on the blubbing. 'Sharon she's coming up see you and your Kelly and little Danny,' she went. 'All come up visit you. Wah!'

'Jesus Christ Mum,' I went, 'you got to? Sure know how to cheer a geezer up eh? Never ought to be you blubbing anyhow, supposed to be me facing the sentence, know what I mean? Jesus Mum.'

Sitting there on visits two feet away the next table, right under some screw me being on a murder charge. Real intimate it was. Then I could feel my jam pies start leaking too. Do without that.

'What you do it for Nicky?'

'Fuck's sake Mum. Never had no choice. Was a ruck, know what I mean? Read the paper, see how it went down.'

'What you mean how it went down? All I know is you wasted the geezer. What you doin' carrying a knife anyway?'

'Everyone carries a sticker Mum.' Got too weary to explain, never had the energy. 'Ask someone tell you about it, Jimmy or Rameez or Sherry give you the knockings only do me a favour, Mum, eh.'

She left off a bit on that only then she started off blubbing again, half of visits clocking her. 'I never minded a bit of tea-leafing,' she goes, 'you got to expect it off kids and you had a few scraps, like, only you never got in no real violence, know what I mean?'

I drank a bit of coffee, hoped I kept it down this time. Waited a bit while she mopped up.

'So how about if it was an accident Mum, make you feel better?'

'Eh?'

'Story goes it was an accident. Seen a brief already reckons I got a chance. You mind having a con in the family serving an accident?'

She shifted round her seat, puffed on the cig and thought on. 'Well that ain't quite so bad I suppose.' Thought on some more. 'Accident eh? I dare say. Only

I never wanted no violence Nicky like it's all violence these days innit?'

Time she finished the visit she was mopped up and yakking on how they were putting the rents up and that Shithead he barely got the dosh for petrol. Never told her you still got a few years on an accident, let her find that one out in due course.

Chapter Eleven

A sian Centre was jumping.
Packed to the ceiling. Never knew how many they got in there that night, forget fire regulations only keep taking the dosh. Early on Indian music then ragga on the dancing, DJ out of Forest Gate knew the sounds. Food and soft drinks like never enough, then Es and ganja circulating. No crack no matter what we said in the word, never wanted it getting out of hand, quite enough to think on. Rameez and the posse went round checking, find crack and it was cutting time. Anyway it was us supposed to be dealers.

Packed to the ceiling.

Five to get in and four went the charities, only we promised them five hundred bodies so after that we kept all the dosh. Meant £2,000 up the charities, and the churches did the food and drink brought in a lot more. Started at seven. Quiet till eight just families, then it was hopping.

Neighbours were all there off Priory Court then there

was some off the estate and the Billet. ''Ullo Mrs Ahmed 'ullo Mr Donovan 'ullo Mr Mohammed 'ullo Mrs Valentine,' I goes. ''Ullo Nicky,' they all go, 'nice to see you son, this very nice do you putting on. Make plenty dosh we hope.' 'Hope so too,' I goes. 'Get the little beggars treated eh?' Move on to the rest. Nervous as fuck. What happening?

Nine o'clock all the Asian birds go home. Fucking beautiful birds some of them, got to feel a few at school only a feel's all you get unless you get it before nine o'clock. 'Bye bye Nicky bye bye Javed bye bye Rameez,' they go, waving. 'Very nice do we all enjoyed the music nice dance bye bye.' Get home probably do their college homework. Asian geezers fucking mad now, want to get their end away got to start all over again on the white birds. Black geezers coming in now, looking round, looking cool, polite while their mums and dads there. White birds there already, wanting booze, got to make do orange squash and Es, getting in a dance before the sex starts. White geezers still down the boozers get in about ten, then they don't like it still get back before closing.

Packed.

Ten o'clock and the old biddies getting on home. Church bosses staying the end only everyone else reckoned they got their rocks off now, went back clock the news. Sounds got louder, dancing got closer. Black geezers getting sexy, black and white birds getting up close. White geezers came in, paid up, looking action, soon getting edgy.

All of us got there early, been there all night. Rameez he was good as gold, everyone in line, not a stabbing all night up to now. Patrolled the area even outside, taking care on deals. Got about ten his posse. Dressed them all in black supercool. Edgy as fuck too only under control.

Us from the meeting we were a shambles beside Rameez. Everyone there though except one accident, everyone did their bit. This was serious business no fuck-ups. Giros were done. Marty Fisherman and that Tina got nicked after a few only they got bailed. Kevin never got spotted. Others kept clean, their bunch of giros no problems. Wayne Sapsford got a bit carried away on the car phones, handed over thirty only kept on got nicked. Already on bail so he was down Feltham, sent a message reckoned sorry he fucked up, got to manage without.

Darren and Elvis lifted a few videos and twenty stack systems up the warehouse, never got them all in the motor had to go back second helping. Retailed them two days, all paid up.

Sean and me we did two nights Walthamstow and Ilford, quality gear only, took no chances getting nicked. Shirts and suits round the snooker clubs no problem.

We paid off Rameez day before, all of it upfront knew we could rely on him man of his word. Then we all took our cut set some aside for Wayne. Then Kevin and me we went round cashed a few giros he still got when the others got nicked. Never cashed the ones made out birds' names only he still had some spares.

Told Kevin put it away safe. Mine was well hid up. Cash.

We were all there and ready. Except Wayne of course he was up Feltham.

Place was on edge. Could feel it waiting to happen.

They came ten thirty.

Paulette and Salim were on the door. Paulette's little sister Tasha down the street watching out one way, Salim's little cousin Adil looking out the other. And all their mates, got the school help out.

Eight motors turned the corner, four in one way, four the other up the village. Like two funerals only they never used BMWs on funerals. Stopped middle of the street. We heard already. We were shitting now.

Four geezers climbed out each motor, left a driver in. They never ran in the Centre only they never waited clock the weather neither. They walked there brisk for the business. Thirty-two geezers and sawn-offs in every mitt. Eight of them went round the back.

Fuck.

I already got the dosh out, sent Sharon home with it. Meant you lost a few notes on the drinks only there was bigger things out there now, fuck the dosh. And get Sharon out.

'Scuse me mister five pounds each get in here,' went Paulette. 'Charity do everyone got to pay.'

Bit cheeky on a geezer holding a sawn-off, bit cheeky and not very smart. Geezer swung it, broke her jaw. She went down crying slowly. Geezer stepped on past her.

So twenty-four geezers came in the front. Down the bit of passage broke in the hall and fanned out on the wall. Eight came in the back made their moves on that wall. White geezers all of them, hard men out Canning Town except Errol News. Andrew Okema still convalescing. Micky Dressler I never reckoned only got to be there somewhere. They all got inside. Them and about seven hundred ravers.

They fired up the ceiling catch people's attention. They caught it.

They aimed on putting the fear up. They put the fear up. It was noisy. It was like a bomb went off.

Then they fired up the deck, DJ got it in the hand, sounds went crazy then went dead.

One moment there was total silence.

Then there was fucking zoo.

Everyone screaming. There were birds screaming out of fear, there were geezers screaming out of fear, there were geezers boiling ready winding up for the rucking. This was what we all waited for, this was it, only this was out our league. Me I was shitless.

We had our squad out of the middle already. Rameez and his posse lined the walls along the side, the rest of us got out of the bunch. We reckoned when we closed in the rest of Walthamstow got to follow. Froze if we froze, joined in we closed in. We reckoned it that way anyhow.

Canning Town they never searched out anyone special like me or Jimmy Foley. They reckoned we put the word out on the gear, we set it up we were the lord, so now they teach us serious lessons. So now they start the shooting. Shoot anyone wanted to argue, otherwise shoot anyone else. Clear the floor.

Only they reckoned it wrong.

Floor was packed hundreds over capacity. Floor was out of it, terrified, only no one got away because no one got an exit. So the crowd was on them no choice, and geezers never had the space. Closed them down fast before they even got the shooters up.

They got plenty other weapons aside from shooters only we had too, and we had seven hundred heads never liked them, frightened or not. So we stopped them on the sawn-offs it was no worries on the rest.

It started.

Rameez was at it, never had the fear. Flung himself on the closest not a moment waiting, closed him down. Aftab and Afzal piled on, buried him. Javed took the next a rice flail on the shoulder, made a serious mess, the shoulder went limp. Third geezer just lifted, shot at Javed, missed, hit some bird in the arm everyone screamed again. Bird passed out.

Elvis was there with a machete. Stopped the geezer's gun arm right off. No fire no more. Geezer roared howling blood on his face, staggered off one side.

Then it was all in close, sweat and stabbing. Seven hundred bodies, moving round, clutching grabbing fighting off. You saw a viz, not local, you ripped it. Canning Town never reckoned who was enemy – everyone was enemy.

Dean Longmore next to me always carried a chisel, found it useful now, tore up a geezer's hooter. I glassed him round the chin then he was on me, tore me down and I was under, fuck I was done. Then sudden he got lifted up and some geezer hit him so hard his tea came out his gob. It was Ronnie Good.

'Fucking Ronnie!' I yelled out.

'You weren't never no fuckin' use, Nicky,' he yelled. 'Out your fuckin' league mate, reckoned you might want some assist,' and he pulled me up one hand slugged the fucker again the other.

Sherry was with him. Sherry who was with Vinnie, Sherry I chased ever since. 'Sherry!' I goes. 'Nicky!' he goes grinning, then he got wrestling some ugly shithead had a tattoo on his hooter. Shithead lifted a blade. I chopped him, Stanley knife down his cheek. He roared. 'Jesus God!' went Sherry then he waded in some more.

Everyone still screaming. Noise coming down off the ceiling like a tunnel, like we were all buried, never could get out again. Like we were dead.

Round the back looked shaky then. Brendan was there and Marty only they never were scrappers. Half of Rameez's only not the greatest. Fortunate then all the ravers swayed that way trying to get off the fear, one great body smashed against the wall confused things right up. Then swayed back again left a gap a few seconds. A gap someone could get croaked in so we never wanted space. I struggled out the side trying to close things up only I never got there. Clocked something remarkable.

Brian Dear was there.

Got to be he came in the back. Not often Brian went in ruckings, preferred he bought in his muscle. Now he came along the hired help took Canning Town from behind. Shot two kneecaps and they went down quiet to get their dues. Left only six that side and soon be less. Poach Brian's territory and he could get nasty when the odds were right.

Then next up Brian came something else remarkable meant that end was sealed and delivered. What did I clock? Fucking believe it only two CID out of Leyton. Young fit horrible geezers off the drug squad, DC Martin and DC Tempest, last seen up Camden Palace surveillance on some Leyton pill dealer. Tonight our side. One of them hit Canning Town up the throat on a karate, likely broke his neck. No worries.

Then fuck I never saw more I was under again. Some

kid I never knew got a butt up his gob next to me, both fell brought me down. I yanked the other fucker's hair back then little Lennie Tack was there kicked him very bloody up the hooter then kicked him up the bollocks then when he lay down started on a serious kicking. Then several more Walthamstow joined in including the geezer got the butt up his gob, they started a very serious kicking.

And Paulette was there again, stood up never forgot the geezer broke her jaw. Very strong bird Paulette. Crying out of pain she lifted the table they took the money on. She clocked the geezer fighting off Darren and Kevin and a few more, hard geezer hurt a few, cut a couple. She lifted that table up high brought it down on his skull. He went down. They all brought their boots too round him. He never came up again.

A shooter went off brought a gap then it closed in again and we got to be winning, hundreds our side thirty-two theirs no matter how hard. Rameez brought a club down someone's bonce one less. Ronnie Good whacked another fucker left him cold. Then that Tina was up there perched some geezer's shoulders tearing his eyes out. Like tearing them out. Only it was a mistake – she got visible, she got shot. Jesus. Tina was shot.

There was plaster falling out the ceiling. There was glasses travelling horizontal across the hall, not going anywhere special only it was out of hand. There was blood and sweat and likely piss and shit on the floor so you never stood up. There was the noise and heat and fear. I clocked some vicar get sliced down his neck blood trickling on his shirt. Tina was lying there unconscious. Twenty–thirty geezers on the floor moaning or quiet like a battlefield.

Then I was under another fucker, third time felt breath going out, see him trying to get a blade out then see Julie Seagrave grab his arm bring her heel down his mush. Still got her heels on. I rolled clear feeling lucky. Owed Julie a big one.

I staggered off down the wall. Stumbled over something, looked down and it was a head. Only a head.

Went gasping on up the wall and Christ I was sobbing now. I was knackered I was finished and I had the fear. I never wanted any more I wanted to go home it was out of control. That head.

Then I clocked him.

He just came in like the lord off the door. Reckoned he came in to mop up, clock the scenery, check it all went down like the plan. Never reckoned the way it turned out.

Got to be the mastermind, the one got Micky and Andrew and Errol in there. Told them where to go, who to put the pressure on. Told them the channels, the markets. Financed the gear. Took the profits. Responsible for Vinnie even he never did it himself.

Roy Flowerdew.

I ran up at him fast by the door.

'Nicky!' he goes. Then he put his hand in his jacket.

Maybe he puts his hand in his jacket for a shooter or maybe he puts it in for his mobile or maybe he just wants to take notes, either way I never gave a fuck. I stabbed him.

'You hit me!' he goes.

He reckons I just punched him under the heart. Maybe wonders why my hand still there. Then he looks puzzled. Then he opens his gob. Then he dies. Then just behind him runs in Marigold.

Then just behind her runs in about a thousand Old
Bill.

◆

'Marigold no!' I shouted.

'Nicky what's happening here, what's happening?' she
cried out. 'This is crazy, what's happening here?'

Old Bill ran past. Marigold was there standing up open,
could get smacked. There were drivers outside, there was
anyone inside. I ran up grabbed her and outside away.
Round a corner out of range. She never even reckoned
what was happening.

'Nicky! Nicky!'

'Jesus Marigold you never ought to come here. What
you doing?'

'I just got worried, you said you were running this gig
you and your mates, I thought there might be trouble for
all of you. Used to be your teacher remember, kept you
all out of mischief? Nicky there's blood all over you, it's
not yours is it? It's other people's blood.'

'Jesus Marigold.'

Then sudden I started shaking. Legs went. Tried to
stand up couldn't make it. Threw up kneeling in the
gutter. Threw up again. Tears going down. Knelt there
few minutes, shaking and puking. Marigold waited.
Then she came over helped me up, took me over sat
me against a wall.

'I killed him Marigold,' I went.

Never looked at her. She sat opposite now, never went
a dickie. We sat there together maybe ten minutes. Sirens
and meat-wagons and ambulances and a thousand Old

Bill came and went, in and out. We sat there silent till I stopped shaking. Stopped for now.

She held my face in her hands. She went 'Nicky I'm going to fetch the police. Tell them what happened. Will you sit here?'

'Yeah.'

'I'm going to tell them you killed him. You got that?'

'Yeah.'

'You understand me Nicky? I'm not asking you how it happened or anything I'm just going to tell the police. They'll take you into custody, you know that?'

'Yeah.'

'You all right?'

'Yeah. Only Jesus Marigold you never ought to come here, you could get killed.'

'Well I'm here now and I'm glad I came.'

'Glad you came Marigold.'

'Even though I'm going to turn you in?'

Tried to laugh. Never made it. 'Go get the shite Marigold,' I went.

I sat there quiet. Never wanted to go anywhere. She came back with two geezers. Suits. Suits never fitted. Why they always get CID dressed so bad?

'You Nicky Burkett?' went one.

Nodded.

'You come with us.'

Chapter Twelve

Two dead eighty injured.

Both the dead their side glad to say, Roy and some geezer they reckoned got beheaded. That Tina she survived getting shot, tough as boots. Twelve on our side went down the intensive and another thirty-five normal hospital. Everyone the other side got intensive except two out the back turned round soon as they came in. Every single one intensive!

No real argument who killed Roy. Case I was in any doubt I got nightmares every night two months, puked up every meal first week. No one quite sure the other geezer though, five hundred suspects. Hardly accidental death only Old Bill never charged anyone. Too busy charging most of Canning Town. Got Micky Dressler and Errol News in the bargain, conspiracy to supply, then roped in Andrew Okema. Whole lot doing twice my time now. Got to be justice, I laughed like fuck.

Was up the Bailey of course.

Never knew once you got up the Bailey you got two

briefs. Wigs on both of them. Like they took it in turns the trial except the real sexy bits was the top geezer.

Me I got someone I never heard of was on TV Mum reckoned. Snappy geezer, cool dude. Got to be fifty only went on about ragga music then went up the gym dinnertime. Name of Manchester, told me call him Jack. Second brief this beautiful black bird, Hester, legs like you never clocked and body kept me awake in the cell. Only problem she fancied Jack a lot more than me on account of he was cleverer. Never heard that was good reason to fancy a geezer only no telling briefs. He had more dosh in the bargain.

Bit awkward getting a solicitor first off after I plunged the last one. No great enthusiasm coming down the cells. Finally got good old Mrs Mellow up Chingford always took everyone, nonces, arson, parking the lot. Stood up the magistrates, even went for bail. Half the court laughing, no putting off Mrs Mellow. Then she reckoned best try get me the sharpest wigs in London so she got Jack and Hester. Sharp as fuck the both. By the time they finished you reckoned everyone ought to stab their lawyer. Except them of course and Mrs Mellow. Justifiable homicide.

They never got me walking, tall order maybe. Still I got the slaughter not murder, means you do few years instead of life. Fuck that. Reckoned in the confusion old Roy looked like he was leading the gang on me so I lashed out. How Jack saw it anyhow and by the time Jack saw it that way it had to be the jury saw it that way. Near made me blub too. Waste of young life in prison, misplaced vigilante crusader the lot. Got Jack write it down after in case I forgot.

Six years.

Not bad eh? Mum got all the paper cuttings, video'd the news. Got to be birds waiting every corner I get out. Just to make sure, who came up see me but the *Walthamstow Guardian*. Did a little classic, whole front page. Asked me what one wish I wanted during sentence. I reckoned take a collection the Asian Centre on account they weren't insured on bullets apparently.

Maybe that might get me some Asian bird after all.

Rameez came up plenty times all through sentence He got fined fifty quid, offensive weapon. Reckoned I still owed him three-quarters a gallon unleaded fuel. Turned round and said only way out was I went into partnership with him. Me I went no way. Not unless I got a sister. Meant no way. Never let his sister in the same parish.

Everyone else came up all the time remand down Feltham, plenty visits after too, even when they fucked me all round the country. Kept me supplied.

Now it's release under two weeks. See how it goes. They reckon everything changed out there, even Chingford Hall coming down. Kelly wants me back, just a hiccup Andrew Okema. Danny getting big now.

Still no Vinnie though.

Me and Slip we got plans. Maybe they work, maybe they never. I put a bit beside meanwhile and plenty people want to help me out now.

Got to wait and see.